THE DOUBLE LIFE
OF THE
BATHING BEAUTY KILLER

Theresa Finch

1st WORLD
PUBLISHING

THE DOUBLE LIFE OF THE BATHING BEAUTY KILLER

Theresa Finch

© Theresa Finch. 2009

Published by 1stWorld Publishing
1100 North 4th St., Fairfield, Iowa 52556
tel: 641-209-5000 • fax: 641-209-3001
web: www.1stworldpublishing.com

First Edition

LCCN: 2009936289
SoftCover ISBN: 978-1-4218-9123-1
HardCover ISBN: 978-1-4218-9122-4
eBook ISBN: 978-1-4218-9124-8

Dedicated to my wonderful husband Tom,
who encouraged me each day.

To my sister Eileen,
who was amazed I could write a book.

To my nephew Donald,
who thought it was a great accomplishment.

CHAPTER 1

C had Vanburn paced back and forth, thinking where he should head for this summer. He was ready for a change; the large stonework estate was closing in on him and his two aunts were annoying him more and more each day.

He thought of last summer. He enjoyed Miami-everything had gone well there. Of course, he knew returning there was out of the question.

The estate where Chad, his two old-maid aunts, and service staff lived was surrounded by the mountains of Colorado, in Aspen, known for its wealth and beauty. Chad, however, hated it all.

This year it seemed like a longer winter than usual. He did the usual things—skiing, snowboarding, ice skating, attending some social events, and dating—but the social events and dating most times bored him to death. He preferred the warm weather and the ocean. Water sports were his favorite. He thought to himself, *If only I could leave this place and never come back.* He knew, however, if he left and cut ties his aunts would stop providing him with the lifestyle he so enjoyed and did not have to work for.

Chad thought of his father, but not with any affection or love. It had been years since he last saw him. His step-mother to him was a selfish, unfeeling, greedy woman. He sometimes wished he had known his real mother. When he was a little boy he heard his grandfather speak of a woman in the family by the name of Launa. He never asked about her and no one explained who she was.

The Vanburns were a proud family with four children: John, Rachel, Anna, and the youngest Ted. Gloria Vanburn died shortly after Ted's birth; she had a blood infection, which was blamed on the hospital staff's negligence. A large lawsuit was settled out of court.

Chad's grandfather, Charles Vanburn, had a brilliant mind for business. He built his large empire with investments and in construction. He traveled extensively—the upbringing of the children relied on two nannies and the house staff.

The two girls, Rachel and Anna, were very close and inseparable. They insisted on sharing the same bedroom, so a contractor was brought in. The two bedrooms on the second landing in the west wing were combined and made into a large suite consisting of two bathrooms and a large sitting room.

Being only two years apart, they thought alike and enjoyed the same things, even down to the same foods. The only difference was in their looks. Of medium height, Anna was the oldest with dark long hair, large brown eyes, and an olive complexion. Rachel was tall and stately looking with medium reddish blond hair, hazel eyes, and a fair complexion. Both girls were well educated, poised, musically inclined, and very set in their ways.

The oldest boy, John, followed in his father's footsteps and was very much like him. He had a brilliant mind and a good sense for business. He was the oldest of the four and anyone could see the favorite.

Ted was laid back and did a lot of daydreaming. Making money was not that important to him.

CHAPTER 2

O n one of his business trips, Charles met Elizabeth, who was beautiful and spoiled. Charles met and dated many women, but quickly lost interest in them. This was different. He was attracted to Elizabeth from the first meeting. After a quick courtship, they married.

Elizabeth was not interested in any family matters or any of Charles's children. She loved to travel and had many rich friends around the world. The family often wondered why he married her. She very seldom accompanied him on his business trips and was not around when he was home. But the times they were together the sex was great and they enjoyed each other.

Charles was away most of the time, still making his fortune grow. His son John traveled with him; his wife Clair and three children— the two boys Ben and James and daughter Trish—hardly saw him. His wife and children lived very well and had everything they desired. Family ties and togetherness was not a priority to any of them.

Charles and John were two of a kind; family was not as important as making money. On many occasions they would pick up women in bars and party most of the night. Charles never felt guilty—for all he knew his wife was doing the same. John, on the other hand, is more sensitive, but barely. The few times in a year that he was home his wife Clair had other engagements and the children were involved in school and with friends. Most times he felt like a stranger in his own home. He often wondered why he even bothered to return.

On one particular trip his father wandered off with a pretty middle-aged woman and John sat at the bar alone, but not for long. A busty blonde sat next to him and smiled. After a few drinks and pleasant conversation, they went to his hotel. Rose was funny and lighthearted and made John feel good. The next morning he woke up in a daze, not remembering what happened after the sex. He got himself together and then realized he had been robbed. He decided it was not worth getting involved with the police—it was only money and jewelry. He had enough of both.

The holiday was quickly approaching and John and his father would be headed home. Neither one was looking forward to it.

Christmas and New Year's the entire family except Ted attended the large celebration at the Vanburns' estate; other than this time of year they did not speak or keep in touch with each other.

CHAPTER 3

O ver the years, Ted had gone from job to job. Finally, he had gotten a two-year job building a hotel and a shopping center. He shared an apartment with two other men. They all got along well and had a great time on the weekends going to bars, drinking, and picking up women.

Early one Monday on the job, Ted cut his arm and was taken to Boston Memorial. That is where he saw Launa. She was a nurse's aide, and while he was in the emergency room she passed by and smiled. He was taken aback by her beauty: her long blonde hair flowing, her large blue eyes that sparkled against fair skin. Even her walk was elegant, with long legs and hips that swayed. He could not take his eyes off her as she disappeared down the hall.

After he was treated and released, he inquired at the desk about the blonde. The nurse knew exactly who he was referring to, but said she could not give any information to him. Ted was determined to meet her, so he sat in the hall waiting for her to appear. At 4:30 p.m., just as he was getting impatient, she came walking toward him.

Ted stood up and introduced himself. "Hi! I'm Ted Vanburn, from Aspen, Colorado. I am presently working in Boston and will be here for another year. I'd like to get to know you."

Her first thought was that Aspen was an expensive area and Ted looked pretty good to her. She said, "Hi Ted. My name is Launa Price. I just relocated to Boston from Philadelphia."

Ted inwardly sighed with relief when she responded to him, but outwardly his face broke out in a smile. Then he asked, "May I have your phone number—and are you free on Wednesday?"

"I have to work late on Wednesday," she replied, but with a sparkle in her eyes and a look of delight, she also said, "Thursday or Friday would be great."

They made arrangements for Friday. Ted could hardly wait for the week to end. He made reservations at an expensive restaurant, planning to wine and dine her and dance the night away.

The more Ted saw of Launa the more in love he was with her. She had a small apartment on 1st Street. They spent long nights there making love and planning the future.

Ted was as generous to Launa as his salary allowed, but Launa knew he must come from money and always questioned him about moving back to Aspen. He knew so little about her, but from what she told him, he guessed her family background was not that great.

CHAPTER 4

She was born Launa Ann Price in a poor section of Philadelphia. Her mother was also a beautiful woman and desired by many men. She did not use her beauty and what little common sense she had to her best advantage. She slept with any good-looking man who could buy her things and show her a good time. She drifted from one man to another as they tired of her beauty, only seeing her as a loose woman and a user.

She was a hostess in a nice restaurant. That is where she met most of her dates— she never cared if they were single of married.

One night a group of men attending a convention in Philadelphia came in for dinner. They all looked her up and down, thinking how beautiful she was. One man in particular was very friendly and watched her seating people throughout the night. He excused himself and as he passed her station on his way to the men's room, he asked for her phone number. He said he would be in town for a couple of days and would like to take her out.

His name was Michael. He was tall and good-looking—and lived in New Jersey with his wife and three children.

Nora and Michael had a wonderful three days and nights. On the second day of his visit Michael suggested they tour Philadelphia. Although Nora had lived there for many years, she had never taken the opportunity to see the sights. They had a great time visiting the Museum of Art as well as several others. They also stopped at City Hall, Franklin Institute, The Liberty Bell Center, and the Phil Mint. They ended by taking a carriage ride at Independence Hall. That was Nora's favorite tour of the day.

After eating a great dinner, they returned to her apartment exhausted but eager to be alone and make love. Nora was great in bed and could not do enough to please him. Michael had never experienced such pleasure as Nora embraced every part of him as she slowly rubbed her beautiful body over every inch of his. When it was time for him to leave, they held each other on that morning and he promised he would call and return as soon as possible.

Nora's life went on as usual with the exception that she did not pick up with any other men. She waited for his call. A week went by. It was the weekend before he called.

"Michael! I'm so happy to hear your voice!" she said.

"Hi Nora. Gee—it's great to hear your voice too! Sorry for not calling sooner—I've had a ton of work," he responded.

"Oh, that's OK—I understand." I'm just glad you

called. I'll be looking forward to seeing you—perhaps we can do some more sightseeing. I never realized there was so much to see and do in Philadelphia."

"Yea, definitely. So, listen, Nora. I gotta go. I promise I'll try to see you next weekend," he said.

"Oh, that would be great," she said. "I can't wait 'til I can hold you in my arms again!" She could not understand the feeling she had for him; it was so different from all the others.

CHAPTER 5

L ater the next week, as Nora was leaving for work, the phone rang. It was Michael. He said he would be arriving in Philadelphia on Friday by 10 p.m. Nora arranged to be off Saturday and Sunday so she could spend all her time with him. She rushed home Friday and flew into his arms, kissing him over and over again. He laughed as he pulled away from her, saying how wonderful it was to see her again.

The weekend went fast for both of them. He hated to leave her. He also was puzzled by his feelings for her. He had a good life. His wife was very pretty and they got along well; his children were good students and well adjusted; they had a lovely home, good friends, and enough money. As he drove home he hated himself for being so deceitful and unfaithful to his family. He knew how having an affair could ruin his whole life, yet he also knew he would return to Nora.

The months went by and Michael made his trips to Philadelphia as often as he could without his wife becoming suspicious. He was good to Nora and often brought her gifts. She was madly in love for the first time in her life, feeling whole and happy.

She never questioned him about his life in New Jersey, although she knew he had to be married. She only thought of keeping him happy and content—just maybe someday he would decide he only wanted her.

The sex was great and they were content. He never felt this way about any other woman and yet little doubts would creep into his mind. She was beautiful, sexy, and had a great body, but not much intelligence or concern about tomorrow. She seemed satisfied to live from day to day and just have him.

Michael worked hard and always wanted to be successful. Why was he having doubts when he thought of her constantly and desired her all the time? He knew his wife loved him, made him a nice home, and was pretty good in bed, but Nora was nothing like her. She was uninhibited and wild in bed—she excited him beyond his wildest dreams.

The days were shorter and the chill in the air was getting colder. It was the middle of November and a Friday when the phone rang. Michael had to tell Nora he was not able to get away that weekend. She felt a shiver, wondering if he was getting tired of her and wanted out. She hinted at that to him, but he assured her it was not so. He promised her he would be there the first weekend in December.

About that time Nora was not feeling well and hoped her suspicions were not true. The Christmas holidays were getting close and she made up her mind not to say anything to Michael. If it were true that she was pregnant, how would he react and what would happen to their relationship?

Michael knew he would not be spending the holidays with her and arrived as he promised with arms loaded with gifts for her. She was so excited she jumped up and down with joy. He looked at her and felt a tinge of pain; she was so childlike, almost innocent. He thought to himself, *I should have never got involved, as down the road I surely will break her heart.*

They spend Saturday at Philadelphia's Center City looking for a tree and decorations. A light snow was falling. As they raced around from tree to tree, they threw snowballs at each other, joking and laughing. Later, walking along the shop-lined streets while they searched for the best decorations, they boisterously sang out Christmas carols, giggling all the way.

That night they decorated the tree. Nora thought how wonderful her life would be if only he would leave his wife and stay with her, but for some reason deep down she knew that would never happen, which made her sad and scared.

The holidays came and went. Nora spent them alone, crying and wishing for only one thing in life—to spend the rest of her life with Michael.

By the end of January she knew for certain that she was pregnant. Michael had only spent one other weekend with her since December. He called several times, but told her it was impossible for him to get away. He promised he would try to come before Valentine's Day. Nora sounded upset and nervous for the first time in all the times he spoke to her. He began to worry that she may start to ask him questions about his life in New Jersey and pressure him to visit her more often. She never questioned him before about anything and accepted his infrequent visits—she was just happy to be with him. This somehow was different; something in her voice made him start thinking all sort of things.

Nora could not sleep; she was jumpy at work and felt worn out. She knew what was wrong. How would she tell him and what would his reaction be? It was February 7 when he arrived with the largest Valentine's heart she had ever seen. She clung to him, not wanting to ever let go. They went out to dinner.

"Nora, are you feeling all right? You seem a bit quiet and preoccupied," he said.

Nora responded, "I'm tired, but fine, really." She smiled. "How's your steak?"

He said, "I'm doing fine, but you don't seem to be enjoying your food...."

They arrived back at her apartment about 10 and she went into the bathroom to change. Michael made himself a drink and asked her if she cared for one. She came out of the bathroom wearing a black see-through gown, her hair glistening in the light. She's so beautiful, he thought, and tonight she had a glow to her that took his breath away. They spent most of the night making mad, desperate love. She called his name over and over; he held her tight against him, never wanting to let her go.

The next day, Saturday, they went to the zoo. The day was cold and damp. Nora shivered as they walked around, looking at all the animals. Michael sensed something was wrong, but said nothing. He just held her close, trying to keep her warm. Nora knew that evening she would tell Michael.

They ordered pizza and had several beers. She started several times to tell him and quickly changed the subject.

Finally, Michael asked, "What's wrong?"

She hesitated, then just blurted it out. "I'm pregnant!"

Michael sat quiet with his head down for some time. Then he looked up at her and asked, "What do you intend to do?"

Nora stared at him and then said, "It's not just my baby."

CHAPTER 6

L auna grew up never knowing who her father was. Nora, her mother, existed with a broken heart and still loving Michael. She never spoke of Michael, but not a day went by that she did did not think of him. Strange as it was, she never knew his last name and never asked him what it was.

As Launa grew older she pressed her mother more and more for answers, but Nora could not bring herself to discuss him. She still felt loyal to him and would not tell her daughter that after she was born Michael never came to Philadelphia to visit her or Launa. He faithfully sent a support check for Launa ever month, but never a note or phone call.

Nora lost interest in most things—especially men. She worked and took care of her daughter, spending hours thinking of how her life turned out. She did not think it possible to have loved so deeply and lost it all.

Michael's life returned to normal, yet he thought of Nora at times, hoping she and his daughter were doing well. Michael still had feelings for Nora and knew how easily he could fall into his old ways. He also knew he would never leave his wife and children; he felt it better to leave things as they were. He never forgot the times he spend with her and the wonderful and exciting sex they shared.

In high school, Launa was an average student with few friends. She had become a beauty like her mother, but was shy and unsure of herself. The boys were friendly and many asked her for dates. She dated a few but kept them away from where she lived, as she was ashamed of how poor they were and did not live in the best neighborhood.

Life went on as usual and Nora started to date again, but she always compared the men to Michael. She became so depressed that she started to drink a lot. She began bringing men home after work. One guy would hang around a week or two, and another one would take his place Launa suspected her mother was using drugs in addition to her heavy drinking.

Launa became more insecure and unhappy; she couldn't wait until graduation to move away. In her senior year, one of her teachers took a interest in Launa and began talking to her about her future. He knew she could not afford college and suggested she look into the health field. She knew for sure she would not follow in her mother's footsteps and began to think of working in a hospital. She took classes to be a nurse's aide and perhaps some day even to become a registered nurse. After her classes, she moved to Boston and got a job at Boston Memorial.

CHAPTER 7

Ted loved Launa more and more each day, and she seemed to love him. She was happy now; she had a job she loved and a man who adored her. Her mother continued with her lifestyle. Launa hardly spoke to her or went to visit. When Ted asked about her, Launa said her mom was fine, preferring to stay and work in Philadelphia.

Ted thought more and more about returning to Aspen and working in the family business so he could give Launa a better life. He made contact with his father and brother and told them he felt ready to settle down and work in the family business. His father was getting older and thinking of retiring, so he thought it would be a good idea for Ted to help John run the business. His brother was not happy with the news. He felt that since Ted hadn't started out in the family business, what help would he be now?

Ted was still under contract to finish the large hotel and shopping center, but he continued to make plans to return to Aspen. Launa was looking forward to living in Aspen and starting a whole new life.

CHAPTER 8

There were just eight more months left for Ted's job to be finished and he was excited about returning to Aspen. He knew that Launa would have everything she desired, and that made him happy. It was early on a Monday when a new doctor arrived at Boston Memorial. He made his rounds, introducing himself to the staff. Launa blushed when he took her hand and a shock went through her body. She never felt anything like that and her heart started to beat faster. She ran into Dr. Peter Wells a few times during her shift, feeling light-headed and a little strange when he looked at her.

That night Ted was talking to her and she hardly heard him; she just stared into space and kept thinking of Dr. Wells. Over the next few weeks she knew she was in love with him—she had never felt this way towards Ted.

Dr. Wells was divorced and in no hurry to start a new relationship. One day, however, they both were leaving the hospital at the same time and rode the elevator together. He smiled and Launa's heart skipped a beat. He asked, "Would like to stop for a cup of coffee?"

Launa's heart almost came out of her mouth. Without knowing what she was doing, she accepted. That was the start of their friendship. They ate lunch together when possible and would talk and laugh in the halls during breaks. Launa never spoke of anything personal and kept the conversation light and general. On the other hand, Dr. Wells told her of his divorce and how devastated he was when his wife asked for one. But, he said, that was all in his past and that is why he moved to Boston, to start a new life. Launa thought to her self, *Hope I'll be a part of his new life.*

Ted thought Launa was acting strange—she hardly ever spoke of moving to Aspen. Launa felt bad about staying with Ted, knowing she did not intent to move with him. She was almost certain she was pregnant and told Ted of her suspicion; he was delighted and was relieved, thinking that was why she was acting so strange. Launa felt guilty about not being honest with Ted, but she also felt the time was not right to tell him about Dr. Wells. She thought to herself, *What was there to tell? He never even asked her out and probably only considered her a friend.*

A couple of weeks later, Dr. Wells and Launa were having lunch when he asked her out. She looked at him in surprise and opened her mouth to say something, but nothing came out. He laughed.

That night she told Ted a few girls were going to dinner and a movie and invited her along. Ted thought it was a good idea for her to go. That night was the beginning of the love affair and Launa could not be happier. Ted was so sure that she was happy about the baby and moving to Aspen that he never questioned her about her nights out.

At first it was just once a week, then it was twice and sometimes three. She even began to lie about working overtime at the hospital. By this time Peter was beginning to feel that he was in love with her. They enjoyed so much together and the closeness they shared in bed was beautiful. Launa realized that she never really loved Ted and was staying with him because of her pregnancy. She shied away from any sex with Ted, blaming the pregnancy as the reason.

One evening at Peter's apartment Launa told him about Ted and that she was carrying his child. He was so deeply in love with her that he could not bear the thought of losing her; he didn't care what her situation was, just so she did not leave him.

He asked, "What do you intend to do with the child?"

She replied, "Ted expects me to move to Colorado with him, but I can't go—I only love you. I plan to give the baby to Ted."

Peter felt relieved and yet sad that she would give up the baby. He felt that she would perhaps regret it someday.

CHAPTER 9

The days seemed to fly by and Launa began to show; everyone at the hospital was whispering that it was Dr. Wells's baby. One day Launa overheard some of the nurses discussing her pregnancy—she felt angry, thinking it was no one's business who the father was. She felt that she should clear things up, so she approached them and all went quiet.

"If you really must know, the father of my child is a man named Ted. I've been living with him for almost two years. I thought that I'd return to Colorado with him, but when I meet Dr. Wells—honestly, I just fell head over heels in love with him. I realized that I never loved Ted."

They all just stood still, staring at Launa. Finally one of them spoke. "What do you intend to do?"

Launa said, "I'm giving the baby to Ted to raise. I hope to marry Dr. Wells."

They all thought how cold she sounded. *How could she just give up her baby?* Launa felt them staring at her, but she did not care what they thought—she just wanted a life with Peter.

One night when she was home, Ted asked, "Launa, you've been working a lot lately. When we get to Aspen, you won't need to work anymore or want for anything. I am also concerned that all this working is unhealthy for the baby. How about leaving the hospital and staying home until the baby is born?"

She knew at that point she could no longer put off telling him about Peter and her intentions. "Ted," Launa said, "I think you should sit down."

"Why? What's going on?"

"I am not going to Aspen with you."

Ted stared at her.

Launa continued. "I just don't know how to tell you this...but...I've met someone else. He's a doctor at the hospital."

Ted could not speak, but looked at her in shock.

"I—I never intended for this to happen...it just did..."

Ted found his voice. "Did you ever loved me, or were you just looking for a better life?"

Launa began to cry. "I am so sorry, Ted...so sorry...for everything...."

Ted said quietly, "My job is winding down—there's only three months left..."

She interrupted. "You can still stay here at my place—I know the guys at your old apartment have already rented the room and we've already given notice that this place would be vacated...I'll be packed up and out of here by the weekend..."

"That sounds good to me," said Ted quietly, "as I'd like to see you as little as possible...."

Launa moved in with Dr. Wells. The baby was due in two months. She still had to tell Ted that she did not want to keep the child and thought he should raise it. She called him and asked him to meet her at the local coffee shop as she had something she had to discuss with him.

He felt mixed emotions about meeting her; he felt angry and disappointed—and just a little excited about seeing her again. He could not image what she wanted to see him about and thought how foolish he was to even think she wanted to come back to him—and would he take her back.

She arrived looking as beautiful as always; his heart felt light at the sight of her. They sat in a booth and ordered coffee. She did not know what to say at first and they just stared at each other. Finally she said, "The baby is due in about 2 months. I want you to take it to Colorado with you."

Ted was speechless for a moment, feeling like she only was concerned about herself and what she wanted. "I can't believe you have no feeling for the baby and just want to get rid of it!"

"Ted," she tried to explain, "I intend to marry Peter. The baby would be a constant reminder of my past life...."

Without thinking, he exploded, saying, "Fine, but you will never get to see the child as long as you live!" With that said, he walked out the door and never looked back.

When Launa got back to the apartment, Peter asked, "How did everything go?"

She did not answer, but went straight into the bedroom and locked the door. She lay on the bed for a long time thinking about the baby she was carrying and how she could just give it up. She knew deep down it probably would be best for all concerned and yet Ted made her feel so cold and uncaring. She came out into the living room where Peter was and told him everything that happened and how she felt.

He took her in his arms and held her close to him. "Launa, you are not a bad person for your decision, but if you want to keep the baby it is all right with me. I would accept it as my own."

Launa thought how lucky she was to have Peter in her life, yet she could not forget the way Ted looked at her.

CHAPTER 10

Launa delivered a beautiful baby boy. As she looked at him she actually felt love for him and mixed emotions thinking once she gave him to Ted she would never see him again. As it turned out, Ted arrived at the hospital with legal documents for Launa to sign and turn over the baby to him. He did not want to see her; the nurse and attorney came in and gave her the papers. She held the baby a little closer and whispered in his ear, "I love you and I'm sorry the way things turned out." She signed the papers and with tears in her eyes handed the baby over to the attorney.

Ted had just two weeks left to finish up the contract and make arrangements to return to Colorado. He hired a private nurse to care for Chad until they left. Ted's feelings were so mixed up; he only felt contempt for Launa, but was sorry for Chad that he would never know his mother.

He notified his family that he was bringing Chad home with him, that Launa and he split up, and that she did not want the baby. His father and brother did not care either way about the baby, but the two sisters seemed excited to have a baby in the house.

The two weeks went by fast. As the plane took off, Ted looked down at Chad and wondered if he had any feelings for Chad and whether he would feel like a stranger to his son because of Launa. He decided then and there to forget her and raise his son.

When Ted arrived home, his father was away on business and his wife away with friends—not that it mattered as they were not needed to make him and Chad feel welcome. His two sisters seemed pleased to see him and Chad, and remarked what a beautiful baby he was. They never mentioned Launa or questioned him as to what happened. Ted was relieved.

Ted insisted on hiring a nanny to care for Chad even though his sisters offered to take care of him.

Ted put his whole heart and soul into the family business and became a asset to many of the companies his father owned. His brother John was cold and indifferent to Ted and they hardly spoke. Ted had to travel a lot and seldom saw Chad. When he was home he tried to spend time with him and show him affection, but somehow he only saw Launa in him and felt angry and betrayed.

CHAPTER 11

The days went into months and Chad grew up knowing only his nanny and two aunts. Ted avoided him the short time he spent at home. Ted dated quite a few women and only used them for his sexual needs. He could not get Launa out of his system and thought about her more than he wanted to. On one of his business trips while attending a dinner, a business acquaintance introduced Ted to Faith. She was quite beautiful and the complete opposite of Launa: very sure of herself, knowing exactly what she wanted.

They got along well, and for the first time since Launa left him he felt maybe he could forget her and fine some happiness. They dated for a few months. One evening, while Ted lay beside her, he turned to look at her. "I want you to marry me."

She was so surprised that she did not answer for a few minutes. Then she said, "It's too soon. I don't know you well enough."

"Why don't you spend next weekend at my home in Colorado and meet my family?" he suggested. "That would be a good way to get to know me better."

"Now that," she smiled, "is something I can say 'yes' to immediately!"

He informed his sisters and they agreed to get the family together. Faith arrived as stunning as ever and impressed them all. Ted was proud of her and beamed as they all made a fuss over her. Chad just stared at her and did not understand what all the fuss was about. She barely looked at him.

Later, when they were alone, Faith said, "Ted, I am not fond of children."

Ted replied, "I understand—and that's fine with me. Chad is not much a part of my life. He's being taken care of by a nanny and my two sisters and does not factor into my life."

Ted continued to date Faith even though he knew something was missing. He felt that no other woman could replace Launa nor could he ever love as deeply again. Faith was married before and missed not having a relationship. She was somewhat in love with Ted and liked the lifestyle he could provide for her. They were married in late June.

CHAPTER 12

T hinking back on his childhood and living with his two aunts, Chad felt angry and ashamed. He recalls he was only 4 when they took over his complete care. At first it seemed nice to have the two of them fuss over him and give into his every whim. When they bathed him, both were present. If they seemed to fondle him longer and hug and kiss him, he only felt loved. For the next six years the two aunts continued to sexually abuse Chad. Finally, after his 11th birthday, he lay in the dark waiting to hear their footsteps approach his room, but nothing happened. Days went by and they did not enter his room at night. He was confused yet relieved. They never bothered him again and just went on with their lives as if nothing had ever happened.

As Chad got older he often thought about what they made him do. The hate built up more and more each day. He never told anyone about the abuse, but often had nightmares, waking up in a sweat. Sometimes the shame was so strong he would not come out of his room for days, except for school and to eat.

He did not have many friends in school, so he

concentrated on his schoolwork and sports. He was a good student and always made the honor role. No one in the family paid much attention to him. He became more and more lonely, staying in his room most of the time. He did love music and was able to take music lessons. As he was very good at learning, he picked up his musical skills easily. Before long, he was playing the piano beautifully.

By high school he had became a recluse. He tried making friends, but he thought somehow they knew what he was and would withdraw into himself again. He was still having nightmares, dreaming about how his aunts touched him and how they made him touch them. He would wake up disgusted, thinking how dirty and used he felt. Yet, he wondered if some of it was his fault. His father did not care about him and his stepmother never bothered with him. Maybe he was an awful person and no one could ever love him.

The students in school could not figure Chad out; he was good-looking, smart, and a fine athlete, yet he never joined in any social activities or took any interest in girls. They thought that either he was gay and ashamed of it, or he had mental problems. Eventually, they stayed away from him.

After high school Chad had no interest in attending college, even though the counselors advised him to do so. His two aunts tried to encourage him to go, but no one could change his mind. He hated high school and what he went through; he could not face another four years of the same.

He hung around the estate and did as he pleased, never having to worry about a job or money. For the first time in his life, he felt free. He asked his aunts if he could take a vacation to decide what he wanted to do. They agreed and he booked a flight to Miami.

On the flight he sat quietly and began going over his life and how he grew up. He knew it was not a normal life and wondered what it would have been like to have had a real mother and father, even brothers and sisters, who cared for each other. He felt very alone and as the tears began to form he brushed them away. He then fell asleep and began to dream that awful dream.

He woke up sweating and trembling. The steward noticed him and gently touched his shoulder asking if he was ok. He jumped slightly and with anger in his eyes he answered he was just fine.

Chad had reservations at an expensive beachfront hotel. He unpacked a few things, then headed for the beach. It was a clear, sunny day and the beach was full of young men and women enjoying the surf and sun. As Chad looked around, he thought how much he would like to be among them, yet something kept him from taking part or even trying to make friends. Deep down he knew the reason that made him feel the way he did. He somehow always thought that sooner or later they would guess what he was and how he grew up. So he stayed to himself and grew bitterer about his life.

Each morning Chad would stroll the beach and spend the rest of the day at a deserted part of the beach sunbathing and reading.

Miami was a great beach town with miles of white sand beaches and exciting night life. Chad explored South Beach's art deco district, admiring the buildings in that style of the 1930's and 1940's; he also experienced

Miami's distinctive neighborhoods and enjoyed the Cuban culture and cuisine in Little Havana.

The weather was sunny and warm and the time passed quickly. One Monday it began to rain, so he decided to check out one of the Miami Beach malls. The mall was a great place to people watch. Chad sat for hours watching as families, teens, young men and woman passed by. They all looked so happy, which depressed him more. Just as he was ready to leave, a lovely girl started by him. She looked so much like Aunt Anna he was taken aback for a few minutes, then he became angry. The thought went through his mind that he should kill her. He followed her, and when she sat down at a fast food table he sat at the table beside her. She looked up and Chad smiled; she smiled back. That was the beginning of their friendship. Chad could be very charming if he had a purpose in mind.

He dated Jill for two weeks and the revenge was building up. He saw so much of his aunt in her that he made plans to meet Jill at the beach on late Sunday afternoon—he knew most of the crowds would be gone by then. He was a very strong swimmer and encouraged Jill to swim further and further out. Suddenly, he grabbed her by the legs, pulling her under. Then, he wrapped a cord around her throat, holding her down until she became lifeless.

The next killing took place in a little over a week. The young girl was killed in a similar way and resembled Aunt Rachel. The Miami police had no clues and no one saw anything.

Chad left for Aspen the next day, feeling somewhat compensated for his treatment by his two aunts.

CHAPTER 13

The small community of Ocean City was getting ready for the season. The last two summers the weather was not very cooperative, and the retail stores and eateries were hoping for a hot and somewhat dry summer.

It was still only the middle of May, but Joan, the owner of a small gift shop, looked out at the ocean with great anticipation for summer to start. Her business the last two summers was not very profitable. She was hoping only for business to pick up or she may have to sell.

Joan's husband of 20 years had passed away, leaving her with a fair amount of insurance, the house, and some small investments.

They had lived in a small community inland, but Joan always loved being by the ocean, so she sold her property and bought a small business with living quarters above.

She was content by the water. Of course, she was lonely and missed Jack with his positive cheerful ways.

He was so loving and giving that at first she did not know how she could go on without him. They never had children and her closest family member lived 400 miles away.

She brushed away thoughts of the past and looked around the store, admiring what she had accomplished so far. A few more shelves to fill and some accent pieces should do it.

This kind of business was always hit or miss, trying to guess what was going to sell. In early January she had attended a large giftware show in New York and hoped the ankle chain and toe rings would do well along with other items that tourists usually bought.

As she climbed the steps to her small flat, she began to think once more about the past. How different her life was without Jack! In a mere three years, so much has changed.

Muffin, her Maltese dog, barked and ran around the flat; someone was happy to see her. Her friend Pat had kept at her to get a pet. Finally giving in, she went to the shelter and there was Muffin—her owner had passed away recently. The dog was very sweet and they hit it off from the start. She never regretted taking her home.

CHAPTER 14

It was now the end of May and things were really gearing up for Memorial Day weekend. The season for large crowds usually began the middle of June.

Chad had secured his job as a lifeguard and began looking for an apartment. He intended to find a roommate. He picked roommates carefully, making sure they enjoyed being out at night and minded their own business.

Chad was very handsome and had a great body. He was diligent about eating right and exercising. He knew it would not take long before the beach bunnies would be hanging around his station.

Joan had her shop ready to go and she was anxious for customers. She loved meeting people from other states. By nature she was sweet and friendly, but somewhat shy. She hired one high school girl to help out in the shop; if business were good, perhaps she would hire one more later.

A few doors down from Joan's shop was an ice cream

stand owned by Bob Snyder. He had bought the business about the same time Joan bought her place. They became friendly the first year and remained friends. Like Joan, he was alone; his wife passed away five years ago from cancer. They also never had children and Bob felt lost. Finally, Bob could no longer stand being in the house alone, so he sold it and bought a new one-bedroom condo close to the beach. Having so much time on his hands and always wanting to run a small business, he found and bought the ice cream stand.

He liked Joan and had asked her out a few times over the past two years. She always refused and did not quite know why. Perhaps Joan was afraid of starting something—if things did not work out, she would lose a good friend. Bob was somewhat attractive and seemed nice enough—and both were lonely. She finally accepted his invitation to dine out.

He arrived promptly at 6 o'clock looking very handsome in a light blue sports jacket. Joan wore a sundress with a shawl. They looked good together. He took her to a nice seafood restaurant and both felt at ease talking about their past.

Joan said, "I really enjoy my shop and living by the ocean."

"I know what you mean," Bob agreed, "it's a nice life. I'm glad you accepted my invitation. I hope we see a lot more of each other."

"Me too," glowed Joan,

He was easy to talk to and a great listener. The time flew by and before she knew it they were walking back to her place. The night was clear with a pleasant ocean breeze. For the first time in a long time she felt a small stir of happiness.

A niece of Joan's late husband was going to vacation the last weekend of August. She and three other girls rented an apartment near the beach. Joan was looking forward to seeing Nancy again, and her sense of the summer ahead brightened even more.

CHAPTER 15

C had found a modest two-bedroom condo that was nicely furnished and not too far from the beach. He knew the rent was more than a roommate might be able to pay, but Chad would pay for most of it and not tell him what it actually cost. He did not want to appear that he came from a wealthy family; he just wanted to seem like a struggling law student. He read many books on law and could answer questions should he be asked by anyone. His generous allowance was more than ample to get through the summer.

Before he had left for the summer, his aunts once again questioned why he always wanted to get away for the summer months and where he was going this time. Chad explained he had friends from high school that he kept in touch with; they were going to Europe and had invited him along. He said they were very wealthy and wanted to check out some sort of business venture. They thought Chad might be interested. He distained this charade—as if he really cared what his aunts thought as he looked at them with such hate he was sure they could feel it.

The two of them gave each other the high brow—
they knew from previous ventures that nothing ever came
out of these trips. In most cases, they did not care where
he went or what he was up to. He then explained that this
trip would be very expensive. Despite their misgivings,
they wrote him out a very generous amount. He often
wondered if they felt guilty and if that is why they were
so generous, or if it was that they had so much money
that it did not matter.

CHAPTER 16

The summer was now in full swing: the weather was hot, the crowds large, and the beaches full of beautiful young women.

Chad's roommate was exactly the right type and Chad hardly saw him. Friendly with all the life-guards, Chad went to parties with them; he was polite and acted shy with the girls. He knew just what type of girl he was looking for. She had to be from money, good-looking, and remind him of his Aunt Anna.

He met Carol one day on the beach; she was a plain and quiet girl—the kind he always dated. When he spoke to her she looked around, thinking he could not possibly be speaking to her. Here was this tall, handsome life-guard—and she, knowing herself to be a Plain Jane, could not understand what he could possibly see in her.

He asked her out. Carol could not believe her luck and was very excited. They went to a movie. Walking home, Carol was more talkative than usual, telling Chad about her job and friends. Chad barely heard a word she said and could not wait for the date to end. She invited him in but he quickly refused, saying he had a rough day and was very tired. As he walked back to his apartment he thought, *Does she really think I find her interesting or that I like being with her?*

Chad continued to date Carol, even though he was deathly bored and could not wait for the dates to end. One of his friends asked, "Why are you interested in someone like her when there were so many hot babes you could be dating?"

He replied, "Carol's sweet and I feel at ease with her."

Chad made sure he was seen with her in public as much as possible. Chad was a gentleman in all respects and was very attentive to Carol. He never kissed her or held her hand—the thought of that made him sick. Carol's friends could not understand why he kept dating her and why she was completely taken in by him.

It was the middle of July when Chad saw the first girl he planned to murder. She was medium height with long, dark hair and brown eyes, just like Aunt Anna. The thought of his aunts enraged him again as he thought of his plan to meet her.

At first she ignored him, thinking he was just another playboy. But as the days passed and he talked to her, shy and sweet, she began to warm up to him.

Somehow, he managed to keep Carol and the new girl, Lorrie, apart. During the day he was very conscientious about his job and did not encourage girls to talk to him. Everyone who met him thought he was a nice guy. He was well liked—keeping a low profile was part of his plan.

He continued to date Carol and kept friendly with Lorrie. His relationship grew with Lorrie and She began to wish he would ask her out.

One afternoon at the end of July, Chad was leaving the beach at the same time Lorrie was. She asked, "So, Chad, do you have any plans for the evening? There's a beach party. Would you like to go with me?"

"Absolutely," Chad replied.

When they arrived, the party was in progress. Chad suggested, after a few drinks and some socializing, that they find a spot on the beach and get to know each other better. As they sat watching the ocean, Lorrie asked, "So, Chad, tell me something about your life."

He sat just staring for a moment, then said, Well, you already know I'm a law student. What I haven't told you is that after graduation I intend to join a large firm and make good money—I mean, I don't plan to be a lifeguard the rest of my life."

They both chuckled. He then changed the conversation to her. "What about you, Lorrie?"

"Well, I think I recently decided what my major will be now that I will be a college sophomore in the fall—I plan on working for my degree in teaching."

"Sounds laudable," Chad nodded.

"I don't have a steady boyfriend," she continued, looking at him coyly. "And I'm fond of animals. This is my first vacation with just a friend and I'm having a great time." She again gave him a coy look.

Chad barely noticed. Even though they were having a pleasant time, he could only think about his aunt and how much Lorrie reminded him of her.

Carol heard from a friend about Lorrie and Chad going out. The next time she saw him she asked, "Chad, are you dating that girl Lorrie?"

"Lorrie? Naw, she's just a friend," he replied. "I prefer dating you."

He now had to act quickly as he did not have too much time to make his plans. He avoided Lorrie for the next week. She was confused—she thought he liked her. The next time she saw him Lorrie said, "Chad, I feel like you've been avoiding me. Have I done something wrong?"

"No—nothing's wrong. I guess I've just have some stuff on my mind," he replied. "How 'bout I make it up to you? I know this lovely little restaurant that I think you'll like."

At dinner he explained to her that he was having some personal family problems. He seemed so down that she felt sorry for him, thinking he was a very nice and caring person.

After dinner. he suggested they walk on the beach. The restaurant was on a lonely part of the beach with high sand dunes. They walked a while and then sat by the dunes.

He told her about his two aunts raising him, how his father had left the family and went off on his own, and how he never knew his real mother. As he talked he felt the anger rising in him, feeling full of revenge. He stood up and quickly grabbed her by the throat, snapping her neck. She was dead instantly.

CHAPTER 17

H e stared at her for just a moment, then dug a hole in the sand. He then used a clean handkerchief from his pants pocket to wipe any evidence from Lorrie's body. After he buried her, he made mounds of sand around her and even built a few sand castles from these mounds.

He quickly left the area, making sure no one was around. Back at his condo, he lay on his bed staring at the ceiling and feeling good as he thought of Aunt Anna.

A day passed and no news of Lorrie missing. On the second day, however, all hell broke out. The beach was full of police and the news spread quickly: a body of a young female had been found buried in the sand.

The next day pictures appeared in the local paper. The police found no I.D. on Lorrie and assumed she was not from the area. It was not until the afternoon that they found out the identity of the body, when Lorrie's friend Judy burst into police headquarters crying and screaming, "That girl is Lorrie, my friend!"

Detective Brook and most of the police force began

questioning everyone—from beachgoers to store and restaurants owners to lifeguards. No one saw or heard anything unusual.

At the restaurant where Chad and Lorrie had dined, their waitress was not sure if Lorrie had been there that night—what a break for Chad. He remembered the waitress being in a hurry and preoccupied.

All the lifeguards were in shock, including Chad, or so it seemed. When it was his turn to be questioned by Detective Brook, Chad said, "I did go out with Lorrie a couple of times, but we're just friends—I didn't know that much about her. I'm dating Carol pretty steadily anyway."

Lorrie did date a few of the other lifeguards and fortunately one of them favored Chad. The police knew any one of the lifeguards who dated her could have done this, yet there was no evidence to suspect any of them.

The entire area was shocked and scared that a killer was on the loose. The medical examiner assured the police there was no evidence of sexual assault. Even though Chad did not have sex with Lorrie, he was sure he had been very careful and left no clues. The police began to assume that someone was watching the beach and waiting for a opportunity to kill her. The big question was, What she was doing on the beach that time of night and alone? They had no clues or answers. The news outlets made all kinds of speculation and were leaning toward a stranger arriving in town and leaving very quickly after the killing. Did they have a thrill killer or was it someone Lorrie knew? The police patrolled the secluded beaches at night to see if anything suspicious was going on, but came up empty-handed.

CHAPTER 18

L orrie would have been attending her second year of college. Her family were owners of a large resort in the Poconos. Lorrie was educated and well liked by everyone who knew her. When her parents were notified of her murder, they were beside themselves with grief. They had many questions, but were not given any answers.

They knew the other girl Lorrie was with and asked her all kind of questions, but Judy only knew that Lorrie had dated a couple of the lifeguards and attended the beach parties. She also could not understand why Lorrie was alone late at night on the beach. She said Lorrie had only nice things to say about the lifeguards she went out with, especially Chad. She said he was a perfect gentleman and never tried to have sex with her—he only treated her with respect. The police assured the parents that the lifeguards were questioned at length and could not believe such an awful thing had happened.

Lorrie's parents asked if they could speak to the lifeguards she dated. Chad was calm and very polite when he spoke to them; he said Lorrie was a lovely girl and he did not know her that well as he only took her out twice. He said he was going pretty steady with Carol. Jim, the other lifeguard she dated who looked a lot like Chad, said pretty much the same thing, except that he was going steady with another girl. The police said they had no reason to suspect either one of them.

The police picked up a few street people who lived under the boardwalk; after questioning them, they were no further along with the case.

Lorrie's body was released to her parents. When Detective Brook bid them good-bye, he promised them he would find the killer.

Lorrie's parents held a private service and burial; they could not get over the shock of it all. Her brother Greg and his wife flew in from Texas. They swore that together they would find out who did this. Her brother was four years older and had just married the year before, moving to Texas for a great job opportunity. He and Lorrie were very close and had helped their parents run the resort from a young age.

Detective Brook kept in touch with Lorrie's parents, but he had no new information to report.

CHAPTER 19

B ecause of the murder, the stores and restaurants were not doing much business and the beaches were not crowded. Things stayed quiet for a couple weeks. Soon, however, the season returned to normal, even though the investigation was still in high gear.

Chad stayed cool and calm through it all. He was a bit nervous inside, though, thinking of what his plans were for his next victim. He watched the girls on the beach come and go, but none of them reminded him of Aunt Rachel. Chad began to think he would not find the right girl before the season was over and he had to return to Colorado.

The last week of August was quickly approaching and Chad began to give up hope. It was a Monday and Chad was just arriving at his station when he saw four girls walking toward the water. As he looked closer, he noticed one was tall with reddish-blonde hair. He could not wait until they started back and he could see her face. About four hours later they picked up their towels and walked toward his station. He could see from a distance that she was pretty; his heart started to pound. When they reached him, he noticed her hazel eyes and fair complexion. Now he had to make his plans very carefully and meet her.

The next day they arrived a little later and once again started past his station. He climbed down and gave them a big smile, saying "Hello, ladies. Have a nice day and be sure to wear suntan lotion."

Nancy smiled back, as did the others.

"Isn't he gorgeous?" said one of the girls.

"He's a *hunk!*" exclaimed another.

They all seemed to agree, and made sure they passed him again on the way back. Just as they approached his station he spoke again, this time looking at Nancy.

CHAPTER 20

The other girls walked ahead and Nancy lingered to talk to Chad.

"So," he said, "there's a big beach party Friday, a sort of end of the summer blast. Would you like to go with me? You could meet me at my condo for a drink first and we could spend some time alone to get to know each other better."

"Let me see," she said, thinking for a moment. "Friday—yes, I promised my Aunt Joan I'd visit her on Friday. So I don't know...."

"Well, you could meet me first and then we could visit your aunt together. From there, we could go to the party."

Nancy said, "Ok, that's a great idea."

She did not tell her aunt anything about Chad coming with her, thinking it would be a pleasant surprise. On Friday, Nancy arrived at Chad's condo about 7. He met her at the door and they sat to have a drink.

"Weather's been beautiful, hasn't it?" Chad remarked.

"Sure has been," she responded. "It's been a great summer."

"Definitely."

Nancy then asked, "Has anything new turned up with the murder case—what do you think happened?"

He turned away from her, having to compose himself before he answered. He then said, "How cruel it was...I hope the police catch the person or persons responsible."

It was now 8 and she thought they should leave for Joan's. He excused himself and went into the bedroom to grab a pillow. As the couch faced away from the bedroom door, he was able to quickly come up behind her, placing the pillow over her face. She struggled for a few minutes and then went limp.

Chad again used a clean handkerchief from his pants pocket to wipe any evidence from Nancy's body. He wrapped her in a blanket and placed her in the trunk of his car. Then he went back inside to wash the glasses and made sure to wipe anything she may have touched. He then left for the party.

Around 9:30 he began asking if anyone had seen Nancy. Her three friends said she was visiting her aunt and was probably just running late. He sat at the edge of the water looking out into the ocean. He felt pleased that Aunt Rachel was punished.

By 10 o'clock Nancy's friends began to worry and asked if anyone knew where her aunt's shop was. One of the girls thought it was near a ice cream stand and a pizza shop. They called their apartment to make sure Nancy did not go there for some reason, but there was no answer.

It was 10:30. They decided to get in the car and drive to the section where the stores were located to find her aunt's store. Bob was at the ice cream stand and he took them to the aunt's shop. Joan was in the apartment and quite upset when they arrived. She told them Nancy never showed up or called.

CHAPTER 21

They decided to start searching the beach and boardwalk; they went in pairs and would meet back at Joan's in a couple of hours. Chad also joined the search, pretending to be worried and upset. Everyone came up empty; there was no sign of Nancy.

They called the police and reported her missing, but were told they had to wait 24 hours before filing a missing person report.

It was around 4 a.m. when Chad got in his car and drove to the opposite end of the beach, another location where the dunes were high. He parked as close as he could without making tire marks in the sand. Lifting Nancy out of the trunk, he easily got her to the dunes. He worked quickly and had a hole dug in no time, then he placed her in it, making mounds of sand to cover her up. He returned to the condo and fell into bed, not making a sound.

The next day at police headquarters Joan filled out a missing person's report. Nancy was not missing the full

24 hours, but Detective Brook felt they should not wait to comb the area in light of the other unsolved murder. They began searching the beaches, boardwalk, streets, and alleys. By 10 p.m., nothing had been found.

The search began again early the next morning and Detective Brook questioned if the area where the last girl was found had been searched. They had checked that area, but not the opposite deserted end of the beach as yet. About 12 policemen and Detective Brook started to search that area. Within a half hour they found a mound and began to dig. Detective Brook was the first one to see the blanket and swore out loud, "The dirty bastard!" It did not take long for the news outlets to have a field day. One headline read, "2nd Bathing Beauty Found Dead, Buried in Sand."

CHAPTER 22

The town was in a uproar and police were questioning everyone again. Joan was beside herself with grief. "I feel responsible that I didn't call Nancy earlier to check on her—perhaps she'd be alive if I did!"

Bob tried to reassure her. "There's nothing you could have done to save Nancy. This creep probably had her in his sights and would've gotten to her eventually."

The lifeguards were questioned for hours. Chad's roommate told the detective, "I was already asleep at the time you say she was killed. When I got home, Chad was already in bed and asleep."

Detective Brook turned to Chad. "Did you hear Pete come in last night?"

Chad replied, "No, I didn't. I have no idea when he got home."

No one was any help and could not shed any light on the murder.

Detective Brook suggested they get in touch with

police from beach towns in other states to see if any murders such as these have been committed. Everyone was nervous, thinking there may be a serial killer in the area. Days passed and things were quiet as the police continued to search for answers.

The lifeguards were now gone and Labor Day over. In the middle of September, Miami police contacted Detective Brook. Over the phone, Police Chief Duggan said, "Last year there were two girls murdered here. I'll send you a full report."

Detective Brook asked, "Were those two murders solved?"

"No, we haven't solved either murder yet," Chief Duggan answered. "We also have no suspects and are still investigating."

"Thanks, Chief." I look forward to the report."

The report arrived four days later. Detective Brook was not too surprised about the similarity between the Miami and Ocean City murders. What amazed him was the description of the girls. In both cases two had dark long hair, brown eyes, and olive complexion, and were of medium height. The other two were tall with medium reddish hair, hazel eyes, and fair complexion. As he checked the photos, he could hardly believe how much they looked alike. He thought it could not just be a coincidence—it had to be the same killer. He also knew from previous cases serial killers follow the same pattern and kill the same type of persons.

He called Chief Duggan. "The two girls murdered in Ocean City look very similar to the two murdered in Miami."

"Are they indeed?" replied the Chief.

"Yea, and the way they were killed are similar—having to do with the neck or stopping the breathe," continued Detective Brook.

"Yea—on the surface the circumstances appear dissimilar, but on a more subtle, psychological level—sounds like we got the same killer on our hands using a similar M.O.," said Chief Duggan.

"Sure does, Chief. Thanks for your help."

Detective Brook then notified the press of his progress and how he thought the Miami murders were connected to those in Ocean City. The press ran front page coverage about the murderers in both states. They asked anyone with any information to come forward.

CHAPTER 23

Detective Brook got in touch with Lorrie's parents and informed them that another murder was committed. He had information from Miami Police about a case of two girls murdered with the same M.O. in Miami the previous year.

At this point Lorrie's parents felt they could not wait any longer to get the murderer caught. They decided to hire a private investigator. They phoned Greg and he agreed that was the best way to go. The agency of Patton & Quincy was selected.

Earl Patton was a serious middle-aged man, 6 foot 3 inches tall and strong-looking. He had a very impressive record. He went over the case with them and said he was somewhat familiar with it. He felt that some important clues were being overlooked.

He traveled the next morning to meet with Detective Brook and they went over all the details of the case. Detective Brook assured him that all the clues and people involved had been thoroughly checked out. After several hours of reading and reviewing the details of the case, however, Earl felt pretty sure that one of the lifeguards was involved in the murders. Earl's reason for suspecting one of the lifeguards came down to the fact that both girls seemed to only date lifeguards. He told Detective Brook of his thoughts and gut feeling. He then asked for a list of the lifeguards' names and addresses.

Joan's brother-in-law and his wife had arrived from Los Angeles the day after Nancy's body was found. They had officially identified the body then, and now were arranging for her to be released so they could take her home.

They sat in Joan's apartment in disbelief, wondering how such a terrible thing could happen. Nancy's three girlfriends were not able to help answer any questions and were constantly crying. Detective Brook kept them up-to-date on any progress.

The police continued to comb the beaches from one end to the other, but did not find new evidence. The police also went once again from door to door re-questioning everyone who lived in the area. No one saw or heard anything unusual that night, and could not believe another murder had been committed and that the first one not solved.

Nancy's parents were well off and she was a successful window designer for a two large stores in Los Angeles. She had a few relationships in the past, but nothing serious, and she had begun to talk about never finding the right man to share her life with. Her parents assured her in time she would meet someone and know it was the right one. They thought maybe she found someone she thought was the right man, but ended up being her murderer. Question after question went through her parents' minds.

Nancy had been an only child; her parents adored her and could not wait until she married and gave them grandchildren. Now they would no longer see any of this take place. Their hearts ached, hardly able to stand the thought of losing her in such a dreadful way.

Detective Brook felt sad and at a loss for comforting words. He knew he must tell them about the other murder, so as gently as he could he told them about Lorrie. He spoke quietly and slowly, elbows leaning on his knees, hands clasped, and head bowed. As he spoke, shivers ran down their spines at the thought of this unfeeling and vile murderer still at large.

CHAPTER 24

Earl Patton sat at his desk looking over the names and locations of the lifeguards. He decided to start with the ones in Pennsylvania. There were ten lifeguards in all, four from Philadelphia, three from Harrisburg, two from West Virginia, and one from Colorado. He thought it strange that one would be from as far as Colorado, but did not want to jump to any conclusions. He knew in this day and age it was not unusual for young men and woman to travel long distances for various reasons.

His first stop was Philadelphia to see Jim Landon; he knew Lorrie had dated him several times. He questioned him extensively about their dates and who else she dated. After two hours of questioning and asking neighbors about him, Earl was satisfied he was not the one. His next stop was Pete; he knew he was Chad's roommate.

So, Pete," Earl began, "who do you think killed Lorrie?"

Pete said, "I really don't know—but I'm convinced that it wasn't any of the lifeguards. It had to be a stranger."

Earl asked, "How well did you know Lorrie?"

"Not well—we only went out a couple of times..."

"Where did you go?"

"Our first date we went to Oceanfront Café. The second date was one of the Friday night clambakes."

Pete's answers were straightforward and Earl felt certain he was innocent.

"What do you think of your roommate, Chad, and why do you think he chose to travel so far to be a lifeguard?"

Pete said, "I don't know why he traveled so far, but he seems like a nice guy. He dated Carol a lot and only went out with Lorrie a couple of times, like me."

Earl was not aware of Carol and made notes to check on her. The rest of the investigation in Philadelphia went about the same. The other two lifeguards were cooperative and he felt satisfied with their answers.

That night in his motel he looked over all the answers the lifeguards gave and left the next morning for Harrisburg. The three lifeguards were quite specific in their answers and at ease talking to Earl about the murders. He asked if any of them had any ideas of who could have done such a thing, but each seemed to think it was a stranger and not one of the lifeguards.

At this point Earl Patton was quite frustrated, but still convinced it was one of the lifeguards. The more he thought about Chad, the more questions he had and the more suspicious he got. Thinking back to when he questioned him about the murders, he realized a sudden chill had gone through him. His success as an investigator was due to gut feelings that overcame him when questioning the guilty party. He thought about going to Colorado the next day, but knew he had two more suspects in West Virginia to question first.

CHAPTER 25

As Earl drove the turnpike heading for West Virginia, he kept thinking about Chad; he was anxious to finish up his investigation in West Virginia and head for Colorado. His first stop was a young medical student named Ron Phillips. Earl found him most interesting and knowledgeable about the killings.

"You know, Earl," Ron said, "I always had a funny feeling about Chad. He seems too nice for some reason—I felt he is somewhat of a fake."

"Really?" replied Earl. "That surprises me because all the others think Chad is a nice guy incapable of murder. Can you explain yourself further?"

Ron thought for a while. "No, there's nothing I can really pinpoint. It was just a feeling."

Earl thought Ron was trying to throw suspicion away from him, but he did not get a feeling that Ron was the guilty one. The next lifeguard lived a couple of hours away from Ron. Earl left, taking a slow drive through the country. He arrived at his destination early evening and decided to eat something and get a motel; he felt weary and needed some rest.

The next morning he found Jerry without any problem. Jerry was a bit surprised to see him and was not aware that the murders were still unsolved. They spent three hours talking and discussing the summer events.

Earl asked, "What do you think of Chad?"

Jerry said, "He's an ok guy, but a bit strange."

"Why do you say that?"

"Well," Jerry explained, "he always had money to spend. I never knew why he wanted to be a lifeguard, because he acted as if he came from money. If you have that kind of money, why would you want to work at all—let alone for lifeguard pay?"

"Hmmm...never thought about that...," Earl mused. This put more doubt in his mind about Chad. Earl then asked, "Did you know Carol and anything about Chad's relationship with her?"

Jerry said, "It seemed like an unlikely match and all the lifeguards agreed. I'm not pointing fingers at anyone, but if any of the lifeguards did the murders, it would most likely be Chad."

This really confirmed Earl's gut feeling, so he decided to wire the police in Colorado and get what information he could on Chad Vanburn and family. He then contacted Lorrie's family with a update and told them his last stop would be Colorado. They wanted to know if he had any suspects and he told them only one, but could not confirm anything yet.

The report that Earl received from the police in Colorado was a bit of a surprise, but in many ways it made him understand Chad more. He did indeed come from wealth and was raised by two old maid aunts and the staff. He had no father or mother figure to guide him—he never knew his real mother—and had no responsibility in life. He never held a job and was given everything he needed, except love and guidance. As Earl lay in the dark motel room, he tried to picture Chad's life: a father who traveled all the time, a stepmother who never cared for him, and relatives who only seemed concerned about themselves. He felt sorry in a way for Chad—how insecure and unloved he must have felt his whole life. Suddenly an idea popped into Earl's mind: Did Chad hate his two aunts? Did they mistreat him—and he was seeking revenge? He made a note to get pictures of them.

CHAPTER 26

The next morning he left for Atlantic City; he wanted to locate Carol. Detective Brook gave him Carol's address and phone number; Earl called her and asked to meet with her the next morning.

Carol arrived on time and Earl ordered coffee—as everyone had said, she was a quiet, pleasant, plain girl.

"Chad and I did date pretty steadily," she explained, "but in the romance department—well, there was none. Chad never even tried to kiss me or hold my hand."

Earl thought that a bit odd, but if Chad hated women, then it would make sense.

Carol continued. "Chad just left without a word—I was very hurt. I didn't even know where he lived. He never discussed anything personal with me and I never asked—I guess I was afraid he wouldn't take me out again...."

Earl asked, "Do you think Chad would ever be capable of murder?"

She stared at him with disbelief. Earl explained, "I've questioned all the other lifeguards and I'll be headed to Colorado to question Chad." He did not want to upset her more by telling her of his suspicion.

The next day the pictures of Chad's two aunts arrived. As Earl studied them, he saw what he was looking for. Two of the murdered girls resembled Aunt Anna and the other two looked like Aunt Rachel. He thought of calling Detective Brook, but instead he went to the detective's office. Detective Brook was amazed at the resemblance and congratulated Earl on his good work.

Now the real task would begin—proving Chad guilty.

CHAPTER 27

C had lay on the bed in his most luxurious bedroom staring at the ceiling, his thoughts going back to Ocean City and how he enjoyed his summer there. He was happy that he once again got his revenge on his two aunts. He never felt remorse or guilt for his killings—after all, his aunts deserved being punished. He did not reason that the girls he killed did not have anything to do with his two aunts' treatment of him.

He was bored and thought of going skiing. Suddenly the thought hit him: maybe someone on the slopes would look like Aunt Anna or Aunt Rachel! He wondered if he could take a chance so close to home, but who would ever suspect him? He could make it look like a accident and still get his satisfaction. The more he thought about it, the more excited he became.

The next day he informed his aunts he was going skiing and needed some extra money. He did not stay in Aspen, but drove to Vail. The first hotel he checked had a vacancy due to a last-minute cancellation. He changed clothes and headed to the slopes. As he watched the many girls skiing, he was disappointed as none looked like either aunt.

The next day he got up early and ate a full breakfast. Just as he started to leave, a girl looking like Aunt Rachel came into the restaurant. His heart jumped as he stared at her. She smiled.

Chad shook himself out of his stupor. "I apologize for staring at you—I thought you were someone I knew."

"That's ok," she responded.

"May I buy you a cup of coffee?"

"Sure," she nodded.

They spend the morning skiing. As their time together came to a close, he asked her out for the evening. That evening Chad was in good spirits and chatted away, telling Fran that he came from a wealthy and loving family and he intended to join the family business soon. He even said that he would like to eventually get married and have a family of his own. Fran was impressed, thinking, *How sincere and nice he is.*

The evening had gone well. Chad told her, "You know, Fran, you really are a great skier."

"Why, thank you, Chad. I guess all those lessons I took paid off."

"How'd you like to try to higher slopes tomorrow?" he suggested.

"Sure," Fran replied.

Chad knew these slopes would be less crowded and he might be able to cause her to have an accident. To his surprise, the crowd was large and he never had a opportunity to try anything. The next day Fran could not meet Chad during the day because she had some business to take care of. He suggested they go night skiing and she agreed.

The slopes were not very crowded, so Chad figured this was his chance. When they reached the top, Chad said he had an idea that would be fun. He would go to the left and Fran to the right and at a certain point they would meet. He told her to push off first and he would give her a small start. She did so.

Chad went to the left for a distance, but then he cut to the right and came up alongside of her, pushing her further to the right. As she swayed trying to gain control, a look of fright and surprise came into her eyes. She screamed several times, then lost complete control, slamming into a tree.

Chad stared down at her mangled body. Then he made sure she had no pulse. He continued down the slope to get help. After being questioned, he was free to go. The police concluded it was a terrible accident. Chad took a shower and ordered his meal in. He felt good.

CHAPTER 28

E arl met with Detective Brook the next day and they went over the details of the murders. Earl sat for hours going over the police reports and everyone's answers pertaining to the case. Everything seemed in order, but Earl had a gut feeling that he was missing some important clue. He knew he had to find some answers before he left for Colorado and that Chad was the murderer, so he concentrated on all the information he had on him.

He figured Lorrie was killed at the location where she was buried, but what about Nancy? She was wrapped in a blanket—probably killed earlier and brought to the dunes to be buried. He then decided to see if Chad had a car and how far his condo was from the dunes. After checking several rental agencies, he found out Chad rented from a small local agency.

Detective Brook accompanied him to the rental place and together they went over each inch of the car. Earl was the one to find a very small fragment of what looked like it could be from a cloth or blanket. The blanket that Nancy was wrapped in was back at police headquarters and in no time they had a match. Finally, Earl was confident with the pictures of the four murdered girls, the aunts' pictures, and now this new evidence, he could build a case.

He phoned Lorrie's parents informing them of the new development and that he was leaving for Colorado in the morning. Lorrie's parents were happy to hear that perhaps now the murderer would be caught. Nothing would ever ease their pain or bring Lorrie back, but at least justice would be served. Detective Brook called Nancy's parents with an update. They held each other and cried, grateful to hear closure was in sight.

Earl notified the Aspen Police Department of his findings and the evidence against Chad. They were shocked, finding it hard to believe—after all, the Vanburns were very well known in Aspen and never had any scandals or problems with the authorities. Some of the neighbors thought the two aunts were a bit odd, but to have a murderer in the family was another story.

The police arrived at the Vanburns' home with a warrant for Chad's arrest in the murders of Lorrie and Nancy. Glaring at them, Chad said, "You're all crazy! You won't be able to prove any of these accusations."

His two aunts were livid. Aunt Anna exclaimed, "Why, our nephew could never kill anyone!"

Aunt Rachel went up to the arresting officer and said, "How dare you come to our home and sully the Vanburn name? We'll hire the best defense attorney in the country."

The district attorney and Earl worked closely together to build a strong case. Earl understood Chad and the strong feelings he harbored against his two aunts. With that in mind, the case was built on his revenge against them. The D.A. and Earl knew they could bring out the anger and hate he felt for them with the right questions. As the case progressed, Chad became more and more nervous. He would break down, cursing the D.A. and accusing Earl of making up stories. The Vanburn family stood behind Chad, insisting he was innocent.

The D.A. finally had his day in court. He pushed all the right buttons, getting Chad so upset that he stood up screaming at his two aunts: "It's all your fault—you made me ashamed by sexually abusing me as a child! I had to get back at you! Don't you understand? It's you, Aunt Anna, and you, Aunt Rachel, whom I killed."

CHAPTER 29

C had was found guilty on both counts of murder in the first degree. As he was being led out of the courtroom, he glared at his father, grandfather, and the rest of the Vanburn family.

Charles Vanburn was in shock not only about the two murders, but also the disgrace that Anna and Rachel brought to the Vanburn name. He turned around to where they were sitting. With anger and disgust in his voice he shouted at them, "You both are to immediately leave the family estate and never return again. I am disowning you and will never acknowledge you as my daughters!"

They both sat quietly and hung their heads, not looking at anyone. Ted sat rigid and ashamed, but at the same time he had no feelings toward Chad. He did, however, feel animosity toward Anna and Rachel.

Charles glanced at Ted and felt he could not point blame at him as he himself was no better at raising his own children.

John and his family just stared straight ahead, not

looking to the right or left.

The reporters gathered outside the courtroom were just waiting to throw a hundred questions at each family member. As they left the courthouse, each one answered the same way: "No comment."

Anna and Rachel ran after their father screaming, "What will we do? How can we live?"

As unequivocally and cold as he could, he answered, "You can pick up your personal belongings—where you go or how you live is no concern of mine."

As Charles was driving home, he felt sorry and somewhat obligated to his grandson. He decided to hire his own private investigator to see if he could find some new evidence to appeal the case.

CHAPTER 30

The judge ordered Chad to be evaluated by a psychiatrist. Chad was uncooperative and hostile toward Dr. Curry.

"I've told you, he insisted, "I was tricked by the D.A. and that Patton fellow is evil and just wants to make money!"

"What about your two aunts?" Dr. Curry had asked similar questions about his aunts throughout the evaluation, but each time Chad clammed up.

"Would you like to tell me about your family life in general? How do you enjoy living in luxury and never having to work?"

Chad said, "It's none of your business how I live—and as for not working—why should I work when there's plenty of money available?"

Dr. Curry next asked, "Who was the one in the family who gave you money when you asked?"

He just turned away and did not answer him.

Chad was in a high-security section of the mental hospital. All his meals were served in his room. He constantly complained about the food and being confined to his room.

The next session that Dr. Curry had with Chad did not go any better.

Dr. Curry knew about Chad's childhood and the hate he felt for his two aunts—it would be a long time for Chad to heal. He spoke with Earl several times, knowing that Earl knew Chad better than any of his family members did. Earl sent him his notes on the case. As Dr. Curry studied them, he was more convinced that Chad was a very sick young man.

The weeks passed and Dr. Curry was not making any progress with Chad. The sessions were making Chad more angry and resentful toward Dr. Curry, so he decided to let Chad have a week off to rest and relax.

CHAPTER 31

C had's room was nicely furnished with a large screen TV, a radio, and a computer—among many other things to entertain him. The room was monitored at all times and Dr. Curry could watch Ted's actions each day. Chad did a lot of pacing and talking to himself. He repeated many times over that no one knew what it was like living with his two aunts and feeling such hate. He continued to chatter away about not having a real mother and how his father ignored him. Sometimes he made no sense and other times he just mumbled under his breath.

After the week was up, Dr. Curry continued with the sessions. Chad was a little more talkative, but not about family. He wanted to know why he was confined to his room for a week. Dr. Curry assured him it was for him to rest and relax. This was the first time anyone really took an interest in him and how he felt—this made him feel good and he started to warm up a bit. He never admitted anything, but did comment on how much he loved the ocean and being a lifeguard. He said all the lifeguards were nice, especially his roommate Pete. Dr. Curry wanted to know what he thought about the girls and if he dated any of them. This was not a good subject to bring up. Chad got belligerent with him and would not answer any more questions or even speak to him. Back in his room, he swore at Dr. Curry, saying he was just like the rest of them, trying to trick him.

The rest of the day he sat in his room searching the different web sites. Nothing seemed to interest him until he saw one with the heading "Meet Your Soul Mate."

CHAPTER 32

The next day he refused to leave his room and meet with Dr. Curry. This lasted for three days—but he was finally so bored he decided to meet with him. Dr. Curry was very careful what he said to Chad and only spoke of things in general. He knew he had to gain his confidence before he became too personal with him. After several more sessions, Chad wanted to know when he could leave and go home. No visitors were permitted for the first three months and Chad never asked about his family and why no one came to visit.

He was permitted to sit in the lounge with an attendant. He was pleasant to everyone and even smiled at some of the nurses. One day while a pretty young nurse was walking past him, he asked, "Nurse, would you please sit and talk with me?"

She said, "Sorry, sir, it's not permitted—I'll get in trouble if I did."

At his next session he asked Dr. Curry, "Why is the staff not permitted to talk to me? I spoke to a nurse and only wanted to talk a few minutes with her, but she refused."

Dr. Curry explained, "The help has to act professionally and not mingle with the patients."

That made Chad mad and he refused to say anything more. Back in his room, he started talking a mile a minute saying, *So, the staff is too good to talk to me. I come from a prominent family with money—why do they think I'm not good enough?* He never took into account what Dr. Curry had explained to him. He just kept repeating, *So, they think I'm not good enough—well, I'll show them.*

CHAPTER 33

C harles knew word about his grandson would spread quickly and he had to act on behalf of his holdings in many large companies. He figured the best would be to sell in Europe.

He had his accountant meet with him to go over all his assets. Charles was worth millions of dollars and he knew a lot of work would be involved in selling his companies.

He called John and Ted and told them of his plans.

John figured it did not matter to him; he was tired of all the travel and would end up with enough money to live the rest of his life in comfort. His children were grown, and none of them were interested in the family business. Ben was a success in his own business. Trish was married to a tycoon and had all she desired. James was the eccentric one in the family. He took off after college and moved to San Francisco. He was interested in the arts and was happy living among the artists and gays in San Francisco. Not being interested in money, he only contacted his parents if an emergency arose. They kept in contact with him and often sent money without him asking. They were not sure if he was gay or just enjoyed his bohemian lifestyle.

Clair, John's wife, was also tired of the fast lane and was becoming close to John. Their marriage was better than it had ever been. They took trips together and, much to their surprise, they enjoyed each other's company.

Ted, on the other hand, was not happy to hear the news, but understood his father's decision. Ted's life with Faith was not a happy one; they both grew further apart each time Ted was home. He thought more and more about getting a divorce and living the rest of his life alone. He still thought of Launa more then he cared to and often wondered if they were together and had raised Chad how different his life would have turned out.

CHAPTER 34

Ted continued to think a lot about Chad, feeling guilty for not being aware of what was happening to him. The times he was with Chad he never asked how he was and what was going on in his life.

All the time Chad was growing up Ted was trying to make his marriage work. His efforts and attention were given completely to Faith. She never even looked at Chad, let alone spoke to him.

Now he realized how awful he treated Chad and what a terrible father he was to him. He also wondered about the two aunts. Why did they sexually abuse him? He became angrier and more hateful towards them.

Ted called the hospital and spoke to Dr. Curry about Chad's condition. Dr. Curry was not very encouraging as to his progress, saying, "Chad has a long way to go—we can only hope he recovers. How come you never knew about the abuse—did you help raise him?"

Ted admitted, "No, I was not a part of Chad's growing up. I regret that now. May I visit?"

Dr. Curry said, "It's too early. I don't know if Chad will ever want to see you."

Ted felt sad and wondered how he could possibly help Chad. He spoke to his own father, asking for advice. Even though Charles was flattered, he felt he did not qualify to advise him—he was thinking how bad of a job he himself had done as a father. They discussed Chad and the two sisters for several hours, loathing their actions. Ted knew his father had disowned them and they had left the family home. Neither one of them were interested in where the two went.

CHAPTER 35

When the three months were up, Charles called Dr. Curry to set up an appointment to visit Chad. He asked if he could bring Ted along. Dr. Curry set the time they could visit, but advised Charles not to expect Chad to welcome either one of them. When Chad was told of their visit, he screamed at Dr. Curry, saying, "What do they want? Why should I see them—I hate them both!"

On the drive to the hospital, Charles told Ted, "I plan to try and re-open the case and help Chad prove his innocence."

Ted said, "I'm pleased to hear that, Dad. I wonder if Dr. Curry would approve."

Once at the hospital, Charles calmly explained to Chad, "I want to help prove that you are not guilty of these horrible crimes."

Chad just sat glaring at both of them at first, and then asked, "Why the interest in me now?" Despite his twisted mind, Chad was very intelligent and remembered how his entire family had treated him and how alone he felt his whole life.

Ted sat quietly and let his father do all the talking, Charles went on and on, saying, "Ted and I were very wrong in how we treated you. We just want to make it up to you." Chad took it all in, thinking that he didn't care how he got out of this as long as he did get out.

The next day at his session, Dr. Curry asked, "How did everything go with your father and grandfather?"

Chad casually answered, "The two old bastards want to help me get out."

Dr. Curry, equally nonchalantly, responded, "Oh, did they?" Inwardly, though, he was furious with them. Later in the day he called Charles, saying, "Why did you bring up the subject of getting Chad released and a new trial? Don't you understand how damaged and mentally ill your grandson is?"

CHAPTER 36

C had seemed to appear a bit more content and not quite as angry. Dr. Curry could only assume it was because he thought he soon would be released.

Chad was sitting in the recreation room one sunny afternoon when he noticed a unattractive girl assisting some of the patients. He watched her a while. As she passed him, he looked up and asked, "How are you today? It's a beautiful day." She nodded and smiled at him.

He began to make plans to gain her friendship and confidence. He figured it was good to have someone on the inside as a friend, and he was sure this girl, whose name was Sue, was flattered to have someone as handsome as him even notice her. He thought his grandfather was not moving fast enough for his release and perhaps she would be some use to him if he had to plan his own escape. *After all, he thought, I shouldn't even be in this place.*

It was now going on five months and still Charles had

no good news for Chad. This irritated Chad more and more each time his father and grandfather visited. On one of their visits he lashed out at them, asking why they even bothered to visit if they could not get him out of this place. Chad was not only hateful toward them, he would also not listen to reason, being very stubborn and strong willed. Dr. Curry gave them weekly reports on his progress, which were not very encouraging

Chad continued to be friendly with Sue; as the weeks passed she sat a little longer each day visiting with him. Dr. Curry was aware of the situation and felt it was harmless. They were never completely alone and Chad was careful what he said to her. He slipped notes to her explaining how he was framed and how the authorities convinced the family that he was unstable and had committed such awful crimes. She, being charmed by his good looks and humble ways, believed him.

CHAPTER 37

Sue never really had a boyfriend and longed for someone to be with. She lived alone in a small apartment with her two cats for company. She was hired at the hospital to assist patients with walking, to read to them, and to perform other general tasks for them. She had been abandoned by her birth mother and raised in a state orphanage; she never knew love or attention and yearned for both. She loved talking to Chad; he was very nice to her. Chad, on the other hand, was not a bit interested in her or what she had to say—he was just a very good con man who made her feel like she had a caring friend.

Dr. Curry called Sue into his office one day and wanted to know what she and Chad talked about. She said they talked about many things, but mostly he was interested in what her life was like. She said Chad did tell her that he planned on becoming a lawyer someday and helping people. She found him interesting and quite the gentleman. Dr. Curry warned her to be careful as Chad was committed to the hospital for a reason and she should not believe all he tells her. Chad had warned Sue that Dr.

Curry would try to turn her against him, so she agreed to be cautious.

Sue saw Chad as a victim and not as a threat. He continued to slip notes to her. She looked forward to them, but waited until she was home to read them. Sometimes he wrote little personal messages in the notes; she beamed when she read them. She started to take more interest in her appearance, hoping Chad would notice. He would compliment her from time to time, which made her day.

Chad began to plan his escape and knew he could count on her help.

"Sue," Chad said, "you know I really don't belong here and my father and grandfather aren't really doing as much as they said they were going to do to get me released. So, I have an idea...."

Sue's eyes lit up. "What kind of idea, Chad?"

"I'm going to escape from this hellhole!"

"Oh no, Chad—you can't be serious! It's too dangerous," Sue said.

"Well, yea, a little dangerous I guess, but I will have an iron-clad plan worked out soon—you'll see—it will be as easy as pie!" he said.

"I just don't know, Chad...what will happen if you get caught?" Sue felt hesitate and scared.

"I won't—not with my plans and your help—together we can do it!" he said, caressing her hair.

"Well...okay. I trust you, Chad."

"Of course you can. We'll both be free and together, away from all of this!" he exclaimed.

Sue felt happy that Chad would want to be with her, yet she was afraid. Alone in her apartment at night she went over his plans and thought about each move and how things would go. She worried what would happen if they got caught.

Chad had no doubt that he would succeed and be free once again. He questioned her about her life and if she had any money for them to use once he escaped. He said he had a lot of money and would get it one way or another—then they would never have to worry about anything.

CHAPTER 38

Charles had to leave for Europe to take care of selling several properties. He told Ted to be sure to keep visiting Chad so he would not once again feel deserted. Ted felt uneasy going alone, but promised he would. On one of his visits Chad asked, "Where's your bitch wife?"

"Things are not going well between us—we are getting a divorce," Ted explained.

"I'm pleased to hear that, dear old dad, very pleased," Chad said, then thought to himself, *Who needs women except to use them?* He never thought about the killings he committed or his two aunts or, for that matter, anyone but himself.

After Ted had visited his son, he went to see Dr. Curry to check on Chad's progress. Dr. Curry told Ted, "Chad's developed a friendship with one of our aides, Sue. That worries me—Chad is not a sincere person and I believe he's up to something."

Ted responded, "You're over-reacting, doctor. What could Chad do under the circumstances?"

"He is a very smart, very devious, and shrewd young man with what seems like an infinite amount of pent-up rage. He still remains a danger—within these walls as well as within society as a whole."

Dr. Curry knew Chad was a manipulator; he saw it in the court documents from the murder trial as well as Chad's interactions within the hospital. And the rage—more than once during their sessions the revenge and rage would be so strong that it was frightening.

Ted thought about Dr. Curry's remarks, wondering, *If Chad is mentally ill and dangerous, did he really commit those murders?*

Ted's divorce went smoothly. He swore never to get involved with a woman again. A large settlement was won for Faith and Ted was sorry he ever married her. She had not been much of a wife to him. Riding home from the hospital a few days after the divorce was finalized, Ted thought, *What a mess my life is. I was only truly happy when I was with Launa. How true is that expression, Money can't buy happiness.* He never found another love in his life, and ruined his own son.

CHAPTER 39

L auna and Dr. Wells were happily married, living in a lovely home in Boston. The only thing missing was that Launa never had another child. There was not a day that went by that she did not think of Chad. She wished with all her being that she never gave him up. She was sure his life never would have turned out so terribly and he would have been a happy, normal person. It was hard to understand how those two aunts could have sexually abused him all those years and no one suspected anything. Now he would spend the rest of his life in a mental hospital or, if he recovers enough, spend the rest of his life in jail. The tears came freely when she thought of all he endured his young life. She never met his two aunts or anyone else from Ted's family, but loathed each and every one of them, including Ted. She also blamed herself for walking away from Chad, only thinking of her own happiness.

Most news outlets ran different versions of the family, the trial, and Chad. One thing they all said in common was that Chad was guilty and a threat to society. When Launa first saw his picture she thought, *How hand-*

some and innocent. Her heart ached.

Peter sympathized with her, feeling he also made a mistake by not insisting they raise Chad. Launa knew she could never go to see Chad and be of any comfort to him as he did not even know her—it would only make matters worse. This was something she would have to live with the rest of her life.

CHAPTER 40

Charles returned home from Europe, being successful in selling several of his businesses. He called Ted and told him, "Good news, Ted, I sold off the two steel companies and two of the large hotels. The other construction sales are pending and look good.

"Great, Dad. I know it was touch-and-go for a while," Ted responded.

"How are things going with Chad? Has the private investigator made any progress in Chad's case?"

Ted said, "The news isn't good. Dr. Curry says Chad remains a danger to society and our P.I. is not very encouraging either."

After hanging up, Charles immediately called his P.I., a man by the name of Rooks, and asked, "Do you have a full report for me yet?"

Rook said, "Well, sir, after investigating all the facts and speaking to Earl Patton and many others, I feel the case and the evidence against Chad are very strong."

"I'm disappointed by this news, Rook."

"I know you would be, sir, but I cannot not in good faith encourage you to appeal the court's decision. The facts against your grandson are clear-cut," Rook said.

As he rang off, Charles sighed. *Facts were facts*, he thought. Being a businessman, he understood that.

Ted did not know how he and Charles would face Chad with the news. Charles called Dr. Curry and explained what was going on. The doctor felt telling Chad would only aggravate him. It was better, if Chad asked, to say things were moving along and that it takes a very long time to re-open a murder case.

Fortunately, when they did visit, Chad did not talk much and was very anxious for them to leave. He was deep in his own thoughts of how he would escape.

The next day he asked Sue, "Do you have a car?"

"I always take public transportation," she replied.

Chad said, "In order for us to get away, we need a car. Can you get one?"

Sue thought a while, then said, "I don't have enough money to buy a car."

Chad's mind was racing now, thinking maybe he could get Charles to give him the money. The next time Charles visited, he arrived alone. Ted was out of town on business.

Chad said, "Grandfather, there's a aide here named Sue who's been a comfort to me. Even though she doesn't have much in life, she is a kind and good friend. I would like to help her out."

"Tell me more, Chad."

"Well, she needs a lot of expensive dental work. Would you consider helping her out?

Charles said, "That's very noble of you to want to help the less fortunate. Of course I will give her the money for her dental work."

Chad thought gleefully, *He fell for it.* He then asked, "Could we keep this to ourselves? I don't want anyone to know about it."

"Yes, yes, of course."

"Hmmm...could you give it to me in cash—and then I'll hand it over to Sue? I know she doesn't have enough money in her checking account to cover that big of a check."

"Not a problem, Chad."

CHAPTER 41

After the trial had ended, Anna and Rachel arrived at the house and began packing; over the years they accumulated many furs and expensive jewelry. They also had some investments and cash. As they looked around the estate, they decided to take Elizabeth's jewelry and furs as well—and why not anything else of value they could handle?

Once they packed the moving van, they headed to Denver. They knew quite a few people there and were sure they could convince them that all the accusations were false. Chad was a seriously mentally ill person who blamed them for everything.

The move went smoothly. They had found a two-bedroom, two-bath apartment with a large formal living room and dining room. It also had a beautiful balcony with a stunning view. The problem they now faced was how to furnish the rooms. They knew they had to be careful with their money. After living in the large estate and running it without a care in the world, they cursed their father for believing Chad instead of them. They knew in their hearts Chad had told the truth, but what was the big deal? They both loved Chad and wondered why he hated them so much.

The former tenant offered to sell them his bedroom furniture and they were happy to at least have something to sleep on. As for the rest of the furniture, they could attend estate auctions and check the paper for store sales. Having to buy used things was not their style, but they did not have a choice.

The Denver area was a very social and wealthy place where great parties were thrown and only a certain group of people were invited. Anna and Rachel knew this and planned to break into that circle of acceptability. They had the clothes, jewelry, and furs to attend the parties— and maybe even meet a few wealthy men.

CHAPTER 42

Back at the estate, Elizabeth asked Charles where all her jewelry and furs were. Charles knew Anna and Rachel moved, but never realized that they would take things not belonging to them. He thought to himself, *I really don't know my children or what they are capable of doing.* As he looked, around he wondered what else they took—he was not home most of the time, so he was not aware of what would be missing. Just for a second he wondered where they had moved, but he really did not care. He told Elizabeth she could replace anything she wanted.

Charles was still dealing with many large corporations in Europe, hoping to liquidate the rest of his holdings. He told Elizabeth of his intentions to sell the Vanburn estate and move to Switzerland; she was fine with moving as she loved Europe and figured she and Charles could do a lot of traveling.

Charles and Ted continued to visit Chad, but Ted knew as soon as Charles's business was taken care of he would be moving. Charles was not pleased that he could not do anything more to help Chad and tried to explain what had happened with the investigation. Chad turned his back and told them not to come back again; he did not want to see them ever again and he did not need their help. Charles had delivered the money to Chad the week before while Ted was still out of town. Chad now had what he needed to further plan his escape.

CHAPTER 43

Anna and Rachel were settled in and even managed to find a few nice pieces of furniture. The apartment was taking shape and they decided to call some people they knew. The first call they made was to a Mrs. Sara Dudley, from a well-known family in Denver. They figured if she accepted their story and kept in touch, it would only be a matter of time before they were on the way to a social life.

Anna was the one to make the call and Sara Dudley answered. She was shocked to hear from Anna and at first she did not know what to say. Anna, however, explained about the trial in great detail.

"...so you see, Sarah, it was impossible for us to stay in Aspen," Anna said. "Father believed what Chad said about my sister and I, even after he was examined and proven mental ill."

Sara said, "Oh yes, I can see why you would have to leave Aspen. You poor dears, what a terrible ordeal you had to go through. You know, I've always liked both of you. How are you managing?"

Anna replied, "Everything is going well. We are almost settled in our new apartment and we're enjoying Denver."

"Why don't the three of us meet for lunch—very soon?" Sara suggested. "I would like to hear more about the trial and what happened to Chad."

Anna said, "We'd be delighted!" As soon as she hung up, Anna told Rachel the good news. Rachel was thrilled. They both began looking forward to a new beginning.

Sara kept her promise and called them the following week. They meet for lunch at the posh Brown Palace Hotel. The sisters were a bit annoyed that she asked so many questions. They tried to change the subject, but Sara was very persistent and wanted to know all the details. Finally, they felt worn out. and said they had another appointment and must leave. The luncheon was not what they hoped for, but they felt it was worth it to get Sara on their side.

CHAPTER 44

C had's plans for his escape were complicated as he was still in high security and had to figure how he could convince Dr. Curry to move him. He became more cooperative and pleasant at his sessions.

"You know, doctor, I do miss Charles and Ted when they don't visit me. I feel guilty that I have been so hateful and nasty to them."

For Chad, this was a complete turn around. Dr. Curry wondered what was working in his mind. Chad was there ten months and all of a sudden his attitude changed. Dr. Curry, however, went along. "I'm very pleased to hear you say that. It shows you are making some progress."

Sue now had a car and was taking lessons; she actually enjoyed driving and felt a new independence. Chad told her, "You're doing wonderfully! Soon we won't have to answer to anyone and will be free to live our lives."

Sue said, "I am really looking forward to helping you escape—and can't wait for us to be together all the time and forever!"

Chad had to make sure his escape was flawless; he carefully planned and studied every detail and made many changes. At her apartment at night, Sue also studied Chad's plans. She knew nothing could go wrong, or both of them would suffer the consequences. Week after week they perfected their plans. Chad felt in another couple of months they would be ready. Sue was still afraid, but with Chad at her side she felt everything would be fine. Dr. Curry kept an eye on the both of them, but did not see anything strange going on.

Charles and Ted were out of the picture now and only called occasionally to see how Chad was doing. The sale of Charles's various businesses was completed; he and Elizabeth were in the process of making the move to Switzerland.

Ted found a condo in Aspen and pretty much led a solitary life. Because he had so much time on his hands, his thoughts went back to his life with Launa. As much as he tried to forget, she still possessed his very soul.

CHAPTER 45

One day Chad asked Dr. Curry, "Could I be moved to a less secure part of the hospital? I'm very lonely and would like to make some friends. Only two hours each day in the rec room is depressing. I'm feeling ready to befriend other patients and be with people more."

Dr. Curry refused, saying, "No. Perhaps in another month or two it will be possible."

Back in his room, lying in bed, Chad swore at Dr. Curry, but he knew he had to stay calm and not talk to himself. He thought, *That damn monitor! I'd like to throw it at him!*

Chad's sessions were getting on his nerves, but he remained cooperative and polite to Dr. Curry, except in regard to certain aspects of his childhood.

"Can you remember anything of your daily life as a child? Who would give you a bath? Who put you to bed at night?" Dr. Curry inquired.

Chad just sat there, acting as if the doctor had not

said a word. He still refused to talk about his two aunts—he felt such hate for them that he did not want to even think about them. Each time he meet with Dr. Curry, he felt angrier. It was getting harder to stay in control. He told Sue after this session, "I just don't know how much longer I can stand it! He badgers me constantly. And he still won't move me from high security."

She agreed. "I know it's been very hard, but you have to be patient. Soon the time will come when we can make our escape."

As much as he hated women, he felt differently toward Sue. It was almost like he had a good buddy. Dr. Curry knew how Chad hated women and was curious how he felt toward Sue. One day he called Sue into his office once again and asked, "Tell me, how are things going with Chad?"

She replied, "I think Chad is making friends and that he is starting to feel good about himself."

He then asked, "Does Chad ever show hate or anger toward his family?"

"He never mentions anyone but his father and grand-father, and does not have much to say about either one."

"Perhaps, at the appropriate time, you could mention the two aunts who raised him—or about his time in Miami and Ocean City."

"That is none of my business," Sue refused. "If Chad wanted to tell me, he would."

CHAPTER 46

hree months passed and finally Chad was moved from the high security section of the hospital. Dr. Curry thought it was time—perhaps Chad would now begin talking about his family. To Dr. Curry's surprise, Chad thanked him for the move. He thought being with people more would help him relate and heal faster. Sue also was pleased with the move, although she still only spent the same amount of time with him; they both agreed they should not change their routine. That way, no attention would be called to them.

The sessions with Dr. Curry went a little better and Chad even mentioned his Uncle John and family. "How strange they are. They keep to themselves and only join the family for Christmas and New Year's. I never felt close to any of them."

Dr. Curry very carefully asked, "And what of Aunt Rachel and Aunt Anna?

Chad closed his eyes and tilted his chair back, not saying anything. Finally he opened his eyes. Dr. Curry could still see the hate in his expression. Not wanting to upset him more, he changed the subject.

Dr. Curry's latest report on Chad indicated that getting him to speak of any events involving his aunts, Miami, or Ocean City was not progressing well. The only thing he would discuss was his time as a lifeguard and how happy it made him to be by the ocean. In conclusion, he wrote that Chad would probably spend the rest of his life at the mental hospital. Most of the other patients seemed to like Chad; they spent time talking and playing chess with him.

One afternoon while Sue was sitting and talking to Chad, she asked, "Why hasn't your grandfather and father gotten the case re-opened and prove your innocence?"

Chad shrugged his shoulders and said, "That's how my whole life goes—no one really cares about me."

CHAPTER 47

The plans for Chad's escape were getting closer and closer to reality. In the last note he gave Sue, he outlined the route they would take, eventually ending in Las Vegas.

Sue said, "Chad, do we really want to end up in Vegas? I don't know anything about it."

He replied, "It's a very busy place and easy to get lost in the crowds. No one will find us there, especially if we use aliases."

"Oh, all right. That's sounds like it will work."

"Now the next item on the agenda," he told Sue, "is for you to slowly sell your furniture and everything else that you can. You'll only be able to take your personal belongings."

She thought for a moment. "What about my two cats?"

Chad reacted by saying, "Are you crazy? How can we travel with two cats?"

Sue felt hurt and through tears said, "But Chad,

they've been my only comfort for years."

"Oh, hon, I'm sorry. I didn't realize they meant that much to you. I can understand how much you must love them. Maybe you can find a good home for them. Later, when we're settled, you can have a cat or two if you want."

She nodded and blew her nose with a tissue. "OK."

Chad knew it would take money to travel once they were on the run. Sue only had a small savings and the money she could raise selling her belongings. She now had her driver's license and was getting more confident in her driving ability. She did not drive to work or take the car out anyplace where someone might see her, as Chad told her no one was to know she even had a car. The few friends she had at work did not know where she lived or anything much about her—that's what made her such a perfect victim for Chad.

In his next note, he told her to purchase a map of the western United States and study the route from Aspen to Las Vegas. He said he preferred to stay off the main routes and would need her to be familiar with the less-traveled roads. She was now feeling the pressure of their escape, once again becoming afraid and doubtful that they could pull it off. In her note to Chad, she told him how she was feeling. For the first time since planning this, he felt some anxiety.

He thought back to his two aunts and how they caused all of his problems. He made a vow to someday find them and make them pay.

CHAPTER 48

C had began to think more and more about what little funds they had and decided to call his grandfather and ask him to visit. Charles was surprised, but pleased to hear from him. A few days later he arrived, bringing Ted along. Chad was pleasant. "I really apologize to both of you for all my bad behavior. I'm feeling much better and wanted to see you, grandfather, before you moved. Dr. Curry is really helping me—he feels that I am making progress."

Both Ted and Charles were happy that he was moved from the high security section and seemed so much more at ease. Chad said, "Things are much more pleasant, but I still feel so alone. They don't provide me with some of the things I need."

Ted asked, "What do you need, Chad? Just ask and I'll help."

Chad responded, "If you could send Sue some money, she could buy the small personal things that I want. I know I can trust her completely to use the money for my needs."

Ted nodded, still feeling guilty, and did not question him further.

A few days later Sue told Chad excitedly, "I've received two checks, one from Ted and one from Charles—twenty five hundred each!"

Chad grinned from ear to ear, thinking how stupid they both were. Chad now felt more secure knowing that if they were careful they would have no problem getting to Las Vegas. Once there, he would figure out some strategy to get more money.

Dr. Curry noticed how much more content Chad was and wondered if he made too hasty of a conclusion in his case. In his many years of dealing with the mentally ill Chad still puzzled him; he seemed somewhat kind, yet he knew how hostile and hateful he could be. He thought, however, given the circumstances of his upbringing and the sexual abuse of two grown women, how traumatic his young life must have been.

CHAPTER 49

A nother month passed and the final plans were in place. Sue would steal an attendant's uniform for Chad and he would use her employee's key card to leave the building. She had her vacation time approved and told her friends she would be visiting her aunt in Chicago. They planned the escape after midnight—that was the quietest time and fewer attendants were on duty.

Dr. Curry would be attending a meeting in Denver that week, which it made their timing perfect.

Sue had sold all her belongings and put an ad in the paper for the two cats. Her heart hurt to part with them, but it would be impossible to take them along. A young couple answered the ad and Sue felt good about them. They had just lost their own cat to leukemia and were themselves heartbroken. They understood how Sue felt. They took both cats and promised to take good care of them. As they left, Sue began crying and felt so alone without them. She hoped she was doing the right thing by going with Chad, even though he assured her time after time he would take care of her and always be there for her.

It was the middle of the week and they planned their escape for Sunday. Sue was nervous at work, but no one noticed except Chad.

"Calm down, Sue. Look at it as a adventure and think of all the wonderful new places you'll be seeing. You'll be free!"

"Oh, Chad, you always make me feel better. I am so looking forward to traveling with you and being with you."

She was renting a room at a run-down motel nearby and dreaded going there each night. Once again she counted the money. Between her savings, what she sold, and the five thousand from Charles and Ted, the amount came to seventy-eight hundred dollars. The car was ready with a full tank of gas and her belongings were in the trunk. Earlier she bought Chad two pair of jeans, three tops, and a light jacket—anything else he needed he would buy on the road.

CHAPTER 50

S unday morning was sunny. Chad thought that was a good omen. Sue was at the motel nervously waiting for the time to pass. At 11:45 p.m., she drove to the hospital and parked at the employee's entrance. It was so dark in the parking lot that she felt a bit uneasy waiting for him. Chad rang for an attendant. When he entered his room, Chad struck him on the head with a lamp. He then put tape over his mouth and tied him to the bedpost. Removing his I.D. badge hooked on his uniform, Chad quickly fled down the hall and out the door. Sue had already moved into the passenger's side. Chad flung the door open and immediately took off.

They had to stay on Route 70, a main highway, until they could get to Route 50, a side route. The traffic was light at this time of night. Chad remarked that everything went smoothly and that she did great. Sue was still uptight, but tried not to show it. The night was clear and crisp, and she felt a chill as they speed down the highway. Chad, on the other hand, was undisturbed by the whole escape and seemed in complete control. Once on Route 50, he told her to watch for Route 550, which would lead to Durango.

It was now early morning. Sue and Chad were feeling tired, so they decided to stop at a motel and get some sleep. Sue was uneasy about the accommodations, but Chad got a room with two beds. He said he would have gotten separate rooms except they had to watch their money. They set the alarm for 11 p.m. and were back on the road by midnight.

No one noticed the night attendant was missing until 8 a.m., when an orderly entered Chad's room and saw the attendant tied up and asleep. Chad had escaped. An all-points bulletin was set up and Dr. Curry was called. He said that Chad would most likely be trying to find Anna and Rachel and would still be in Colorado.

CHAPTER 51

The TV news coverage was full of Chad's escape, but there was no mention of Sue being with him. It was approaching the second day of their escape and Chad, watching the broadcast, thought he better use a disguise as his picture was all over the TV.

The Vanburns saw the news of his escape and wondered where he was headed. Ann and Rachel were especially worried that he would be looking for them.

The roads into and out of Colorado were blocked, but there was no sign of Chad. Dr. Curry kept in touch with the police and still thought he was right that Chad would be looking for his two aunts.

The couple decided to spend a day in Durango. Chad, with his blackened hair and makeshift mustache, walked around without a glance from anyone.

Chad bought a cheap wedding band for Sue and told her if anyone asked any questions, she should say they were on their way to San Francisco.

Sue was fascinated with all the sights and began to relax. Chad was amused with her excitement. When she told him she was having a wonderful time and how glad she was to be with him, Chad felt good. He thought, *What a nice person she is. I don't really mind being with her.* This was the first time in his life he was at ease with a woman and enjoyed her company.

After a few hours of sleep, they were back on Route 160 thru Cortez and headed to Grand Canyon National Park.

CHAPTER 52

W hen they arrived at Grand Canyon it was still dark, so they checked into a motel and took a nap. By 10 a.m., they had breakfast and were ready to take in the sights of the magnificent canyon.

Chad explained to Sue, "The wind, ice, floods, and gravity has shaped the canyon's rock formation. Even before that, several million of years ago the Colorado River began to carve the canyon in an area of land that had been slowly uplifted by movements in the earth's crust. The canyon is about ten miles across to the North Rim and about one mile down to the Colorado River. The river is some two hundred seventy-seven miles long."

Sue marveled, "This is just awesome. I can't believe the size of this place."

"Hmm, you bet," murmured Chad.

"And Chad, you are just so knowledgeable about the Grand Canyon—heck, just about everything!"

They spent the entire day at the canyon. When night

approached, they started to leave. Suddenly, Sue slipped and lost her balance, falling over the side. Chad looked down as she continued to fall, her cry diminishing in the canyon's depths. He felt somewhat badly, but not wanting to call attention to himself, he left the area. There was no one in the vicinity anyway. As he drove away, any emotion he did feel subsided. He thought, *Maybe it's for the best—this way I have to only worry about myself.*

Chad took Highway 180 through Williams and continued on Route 40 into Kingman. The next morning he headed for Las Vegas. On the way he stopped at Hoover Dam and took the tour.

When he arrived in Las Vegas, it was more then he expected—he was stunned by how many casinos there were and how crowded the Strip looked.

Las Vegas is a 24-hour city, but also has millions of acres of public land for hiking, biking, backpacking, and off-road vehicles as well as lakes and rivers for fishing and rafting. Nevada is actually the most mountainous state in the nation with its many individual ranges and hills. It is a state where one could get lost in the city or the mountains; this made it a perfect choice for Chad.

CHAPTER 53

C had found a motel a good distance from the main hub of the Strip. He paid for a week in advance and intended to look for a small apartment. He knew he had to dispose of Sue's belongings and eventually the car.

He began exploring the different canyons. Just 17 miles outside of Las Vegas on State Route 159, he discovered red rock canyon in a 197,000 acre area—a perfect spot to blow up the car. He packed Sue's belongings in separate bags and each day he threw one in a trash can along the strip.

He enjoyed walking the Strip, going in and out of the different casinos; once in a while he even played a slot machine. His money was holding out pretty good, but he knew he would have to figure something out once his funds got low. He was not interested in finding a job. *Really*, he thought, *what working experience do I have to offer an employer?*

One solution would be finding rich, elderly, lonely women who were looking for companionship. With his dark hair and mustache, he looked quite dignified and older. The more he thought about it, the more appealing it was to him. He had to invest in a couple of suits, shirts, and shoes. He hated to spend the money, but appearance was important.

Back in Colorado, no progress was made in finding Chad. It was almost a week since he escaped. Dr. Curry returned early from his meeting in Denver and tried to help figure out where Chad would be headed. The authorities knew he had no money or means of transportation, so he must have had help. Everyone in the Vanburn family was questioned, but no one knew anything. Charles and Ted told the police about the money they had sent to Sue to purchased personal items for Chad, and how Charles helped with Sue's dental expenses.

That information made the situation a lot clearer to Dr. Curry. Sue was the one, he thought. Dr. Curry could have kicked himself for not realizing that Sue was involved and that she and Chad were on the run together. He feared for Sue's life; he felt that once Chad felt safe, he would do away with Sue.

A new all-points bulletin was issued, stating that Chad was probably traveling with a woman. A full description of the couple was on TV and radio, with a warning that Chad may be dangerous. Chad saw the news on TV, but felt no threat as the pictures of him was nothing like he looked now and he was alone. Chad thought of Sue and how it was unfortunate what happened. It was a break for him, though, and if things had gotten to be problematic he would have had to kill her anyway.

CHAPTER 54

Two weeks passed and Sue did not return to work. There were no clues as to where they had gone. Dr. Curry felt sad and stupid for not being aware of what was going on. He knew in his heart that Sue would never return to the hospital and in all probability was dead.

Chad found a small furnished apartment within walking distance of the Strip that he rented on a weekly basis. He now was ready to hit the casino night scene and see what was available for him to pick up. He watched some men and woman shooting craps and then watched a few older men and woman at the poker table. Two of the women seemed to be together. He looked them over to see how they were dressed and if they wore any expensive jewelry. He guessed they were in their sixties and should be a good mark. He decided to keep an eye on them for the rest of the evening.

One of them looked up and saw him leaning against a pole. She gave him a big smile. Chad returned the smile, and before long the three of them were in the bar lounge having a drink.

A friendship grew among the three of them and one evening Chad gave them a real sob story about his life—partially true, but hardly revealing the truth. As they were completely charmed by his personality and good looks, he had no problem convincing either one of them of his story.

It only took two weeks after meeting Chad that they suggested he move in with them. Their estate was large and Chad could have a wing of his own.

"Lovely ladies, I would be honored," Chad said, bowing.

The next day he moved in. The two women were thrilled and proud to be seen in his company. Chad felt satisfied and happy with how his life was going. Maybe things would change next week or next month—but for now, he felt safe.